# The
# Princess

## Children of His Promise
## Book 3

### By

### Ronna M. Bacon

Psalms 56:3,4. In what time I am afraid, I will trust in thee. In God I will praise his word, in God I have put my trust; I will not fear what flesh can do unto me. (King James Version)

# *Table of Contents*

## Chapter 1

His head hanging down, Tierney Brown shuffled into the room he had been assigned, not hearing the door slam behind him and the lock click into place. It had become old to him. He had lost track of how many days it had been. He shuffled across rough dirt floor towards the makeshift bunk, the only furniture in the room. The shackles around his ankles clanked loudly in the silence, causing the insects and bugs to run and hide. He dropped to his knees, unable to walk any further. His hands hit the floor and then his body followed, leaving him laying facedown, almost broken in spirit, battered and bruised, not able to rise to find what little comfort came from his bunk. His head raised and he blinked, his eyes red and sore from lack of sleep. He brushed a hand at his face, trying to wipe away the grime that coated it before his hand dropped back and his head hit the floor again. This time, he didn't move.

Tierney didn't hear the lock rasp open or see his captor standing over, a booted foot coming out to roll him over. His arm flopped lifelessly as his body stopped moving. His captor spun, his boots pounding on the floor as he sought the guards, his voice raised in anger and rage. He needed information from Tierney and now he couldn't get it.

Darkness came suddenly, clouds covering the moon and stars, hiding the creatures that stirred with the night. The night birds and owls called as the insects sounded their songs. Tierney still didn't move, his chest barely rising and falling with his shallow breaths. A tiny mouse crept closer, its

—

whiskers moving with its nose as it sniffed around him, and then left, not finding any food near him. Food was sparse, the mouse knew, not much food provided to the prisoners. And there was more than one prisoner, but Tierney seemed to be the only one the captor was interested in. Rumours flew among the men, but no one knew for sure why Tierney was there or what information the captor tried to get from him.

The sounds of quiet, hushed footsteps sounded through the prison as figures moved towards the cells, searching for the one they wanted. A soft click and the lock fell open. Two figures entered, searching the bunk for Tierney before a soft voice spoke quietly, pointing to him. They dropped beside him, a hand out to touch him before he was pulled to his feet and draped over the shoulders of the man. A hand on Tierney's back showed briefly in a bit of light as the figures moved away, the lock clicking shut again.

The footsteps sounded softly as the figures moved to the entrance, paused and then rushed for the gate and through it. The rescuers prayed that they had not been seen, that they had been able to get in and out with Tierney without being seen.

Tierney was laid gently down on a bed in a camper, his rescuers speaking quietly among themselves before one detached himself from the trio and slid behind the wheel, the motor keyed to quiet life and the camper moved away from where it had been hidden. The other two watched carefully, knowing this was a dangerous part of their rescue, escaping without being seen.

Thirty minutes later, a breath of relief spread through the camper and low lights clicked on. The shorter of the rescuers reached for Tierney, her hands feeling over him, seeking to find any injuries. He didn't move, even when she found the bruising on the ribs, the face, the chest. He didn't stir when one of the men worked to release the shackles, dropping them to one side even as he drew in a breath at the raw flesh and bleeding on his ankles.

Larkin Carmichael rose from where she had been sitting on the side of the bunk, heading for the sink and water. She ran the water until it was warm and filled a basin, reaching into a nearby drawer for cloths, and then returning to set the basin on the floor, heading back to the washroom area for the first aid kit. She paused as she studied it, knowing that it would not be enough. She turned her head, her brown eyes with the flecks of amber studying the man they had just rescued. She knew his name, knew they had had to go and find him, but not sure even then why. No one had told them, just asked them to go in.

She turned as she heard James Ascott, one of the men with her, give an exclamation and she rushed back to him.

"James?"

He looked up at Larkin, watching as she tucked her blond hair behind her ears. "Do you know who this is?"

She shook her head. "No. Should I?"

"You've heard of Tierney's Treasures?"

She shook her head. "No, I haven't. Again, should I?"

—

8

James shook his own head. "Larkin, sometimes I wonder about you. He's a noted researcher, studying old manuscripts and maps. Now, why was he there?"

Larkin studied James before she turned back to Tierney. "I have no idea. Let's clean him up as much as we can." She paused. "He's familiar. I have seen him somewhere and with someone. I'm just not sure who."

A sudden shifting of the camper sent her flying towards the floor, a small scream escaping her. She looked up at James, not seeing him for a moment. The camper slid to a stop and Peter Ascott was back with them, his hands reaching for Tierney, even as James shoved Larkin towards the door.

"Out and to cover, Larkin. We've been found."

The three ran for the side of the road, searching for cover, finally dropping down over a small embankment, listening to the angry words and curses and then the running footsteps heading their way. Peter was on his feet, running from them, praying he could lead the men away from his brother and Larkin, knowing that if he failed, their deaths would surely follow. Lord, he prayed. Please, let this work.

James threw himself over Tierney and reached to shove Larkin down, praying that they would be hidden and that Peter would be safe. Larkin's breath came in gasps as she heard the steps rush by them. James finally raised himself and looked around.

"James?" Her voice was quiet. "Who were they?"

James' eyes were on Tierney. "They wanted him. That's who they were." He shifted as he heard quiet footsteps and then Peter was there.

"Peter?" Larkin's voice held a plea for answers.

"We need to move, Larkin, and now. We can't go back to the camper."

James slid away for a moment and then was back, packs in his hands. "They weren't watching the camper. Here, Larkin, you take one. I'll carry Tierney for now."

She looked down at Tierney and then at Peter. "Okay. We need to move right? But where?"

James pointed. "That way. Now, move, Larkin. We need to get out of here and now."

## Chapter 2

Four hours later, Larkin paused at the side of a yard, watching the large house ahead of them before she turned to Peter.

"We're safe, Peter?"

He nodded. "For now. Let's get across there before it's daylight. Dad said he'd have the door open for us." He turned for a moment, his hand going to Tierney's back. "James?"

James nodded. "He's still alive, but how, I have no idea, other than God. Let's move and get him where we can take care of him." The men had taken turns carrying Tierney during their trek to safety.

They crept towards the house, eyes alert, before Peter reached for the door, finding it opening under his touch. They slipped inside, Peter closing the door and throwing the bolts that would hold it closed. Peter headed for a room near the kitchen, nodding as Larkin moved to throw back the covers, before James laid Tierney gently down.

Larkin stood, a frown on her face, puzzlement in her gaze, before she spun, running for the kitchen, finding a basin to fill with warm water. James was at the doorway of the room, reaching for it, as Peter approached with towels in his hands.

"We'll clean him up, Larkin." James shook his head. "No, Larkin. Not yet. We'll clean him up, take photos of his wounds and then you can come back. Dad said something about leaving food for us. See if there's any broth. We'll try and get that down him."

Larkin stared at the closed door, her thought chaotic. She knew this man, she thought, but just how she wasn't sure. She would ask him when he roused. Then she sighed. It was not even certain if he would survive. She had caught the looks between her two cousins and if she was reading them correctly, they didn't expect him to either. She had caught glimpses of the darkening bruises and shuddered at what he must have suffered.

She searched the kitchen she was so familiar with and found the food James had mentioned. She paused, her hand on the cupboard, her eyes turning to the kitchen doorway before she shrugged. She would heat the broth but she wasn't sure if they would even get any down Tierney. She sighed, her eyes on the closed window blinds, her thoughts still chaotic, even as she tried to pray. God didn't feel close to her anymore, she thought. Given what her two brothers had been through, He should be. She shook her head, reaching for the bread and meat, putting on the coffee for her cousins, the kettle for herself.

She paused as she heard the quiet snick of a lock and jumped, spinning around, a hand to her throat. Titus Ascott stopped for a moment before he was across the floor, catching his niece into a hard hug before he set her back, hands on her arms, studying her face.

"Larkin?" He watched the emotions crossing her face. "Are you okay?"

She nodded. "I think so. It's not what I expected, though."

"No, it wouldn't be." He looked around. "The boys?"

"They're with Tierney, I think they called him." She looked up, emotions running deep in her eyes. "He's hurt bad, Uncle Titus. I don't know if he'll make it."

Titus nodded, reaching for the medical bag and supplies he had dropped on the table. "We'll see about that, Larkin." He looked towards the door and then back at her. "Go, get yourself cleaned up and then eat. I'll come find you when I know what's going on."

She watched him walk away and sighed. Lord, what now? What did I go and get mixed up in? I didn't hesitate when they asked if I could help. I didn't know, though, that it would be like this. I'm afraid, Lord, and have been for so many months. I just don't get it.

She stood in the hallway a while later, watching through the open door as Titus worked on Tierney. She could hear his quiet words to Peter but didn't understand what he was saying. Her feet moved her forward to stand by the bed as she watched Tierney. His body jerked from remembered blows and hits, his head tossing from side to side. She heard her uncle's worried comment that they needed to calm him but he had no idea just how to do that. He didn't want to give a sedative to him if he could avoid that.

Without thinking, she sat beside Tierney, a hand reaching for his, the other hand on his cheek, feeling

---

the roughness of his beard, wincing at the bruising she could see. Tierney's movements slowed and then stilled, and his face turned into her hand, trapping it against the pillow, a sigh escaping from him. She stared, a frown on her face, at him before she looked up at her uncle.

"Uncle Titus?"

"I don't know what you just did, love, but it calmed him." Titus shook his head, reaching for his stethoscope again. "I think you have that touch Holly has and what Logan has. Not everyone does."

Larkin finally rose, heading for the kitchen and groaned. Her tea would be cold by now. And she hated cold tea. Peter reached to hug her, sitting her down at the table and placing a fresh cup of tea in front of her as well as a plate of food.

"Eat, Larkin. Then we need to talk." He sat across from her, his hands wrapped around a brown coffee mug, his eyes on the far wall behind her.

"Peter?"

He shook his head, worried for her, sad that they had to include her, but the instructions had been specific. There was to be no one other than their family involved and Larkin was specifically mentioned. He frowned at that. That was something none of them could understand. His eyes on her, he sipped at his coffee, watching as she picked at the eggs and toast before shoving her plate back, her head going down on her folded arms as she slept.

Titus stood for a moment, his eyes on his niece before looking at Peter. He swept her into his arms and carried her to the room she always used, tucking her under a blanket and then just watching her before he walked away. Lord, I have no idea what going on, but You do. Please protect our Larkin. She's been hurting now for months and none of us can get her to talk. Not her brothers. Not her parents. Not the boys. Not even her Aunt Lois. Who can we bring in that she will talk to?

He stopped for a moment to assess Tierney and then nodded at the door, James rising from the chair he had been in to follow his father.

Titus gave a groan as he sat, his phone on the table in front of him. Liam, Larkin's father, had sent a text, asking how it had gone. Larkin had refused to tell her family she was involved and Titus had agreed, wishing now that he had not, but knowing her brothers, it was probably better that they hadn't known.

"Dad?" James' quiet voice caught at his attention and he raised his head. "Tierney? Will he live?"

Titus shook his head. "It's in God's hands now, son. I've done what I can. I would really like to run imaging but that can't happen. We can't let anyone know he's here." He sighed. "Your Mom's planning on heading this way later this morning. I can't keep her away."

Peter nodded. "She's what we need here, Dad. As a nurse, she can look after him better than we can." He peered towards the hallway. "What was that with Larkin and him?"

"What was what?" Titus had an idea what Peter was asking but waited for him to vocalize his thoughts.

"She calmed him, just with a touch. I know Lincoln says that's what Holly does to him and Logan does that too, but Larkin?"

Titus shook his head. "I can't explain that, Peter. No one who has that touch can. It's something God gives people that we don't understand. Medicine can't explain it." He sipped at his coffee, his eyes on his plate. "We just have to accept that."

Rising at hearing a sound, he strode from the kitchen, stopping at Tierney's bedside, hearing the muttering and murmuring, his heart sinking as he realized just how entwined Tierney and Larkin were. He stepped back to the hallway, staring at his niece's door before stepping back to Tierney's side, his hand on the man's shoulders as he tried to calm him. A whisper of sound came and Larkin was there, on her knees by the bed, her hands on Tierney, calming him once more.

## Chapter 3

Four days later, Titus stood, watching as Larkin sat near Tierney's bed, her book open on her lap, but her eyes on the window. He could see the shadows on her face and wanted to help her. He knew her father and mother were due in that afternoon and maybe, he thought, just maybe they would be able to reach her, but he doubted that. Whatever was troubling here was buried deep.

He walked forward, his eyes shifting to Tierney who now seemed to be sleeping in a deep sleep. They had fought long and hard, almost losing him, but he felt confident now that Tierney would recover but what he would be like now, no one knew. They had no idea of the abuse and deprivation he had undergone. All they knew is that he had been missing for a couple of months when Titus was approached.

He frowned. Now, just why were they approached? They didn't do that kind of stuff. Peter was a professor, James a teacher. And why had it be stressed that Larkin had to be there? She was a secretary. He turned to watch her again, his frown deepening. Lord, I fear for her. What has she gotten involved in?

Larkin rose, coming to stand beside her uncle. "Uncle Titus?"

"Larkin?"

"He's getting better?"

"I think he is. God has been good, girl, in that."

---

She shrugged. "I guess He has. It doesn't seem lately that He really cares about me." She turned and walked away, not seeing her mother standing listening, a shocked look on her face that changed to sorrow.

Titus shared a look with Leigh before he shook his head. Leigh headed after her daughter, sitting beside her on the bed and sweeping her into a mother hug. Larkin jumped in surprise and then relaxed. She hadn't known her mother was coming.

"Larkin, what do you go and get involved in?"

Larkin shrugged. "I don't know, Mom. The boys asked if I would and I said yes." She blinked back tears. "It was horrible, Mom. The conditions in that place. I have no idea who runs it, but it was so primitive. Not a real prison." She frowned, a thought crossing her mind. "No, it wasn't a regular jail. We wouldn't have been able to go in like that. So, what was it?"

"Your Dad's looking into that, I think he said. He's afraid for you and the boys, Larkin. We don't know who it was that asked you to go in. The name he gave wasn't right."

"Then, how? The boys wouldn't have gone in without checking it out."

"I know but Titus says they were told not to say anything and had to give their word they wouldn't." Leigh nodded. "And once they gave their word, they wouldn't go back on it. I just don't see how you got involved."

"They asked and I said yes."

"Larkin! You know better!"

18

Larkin shrugged off her mother's arms and stood, staring at her for a moment, before she walked away, heading back for Tierney. Something drew her to him, something she was trying hard to remember, but couldn't.

She watched at Tierney slept, seeing the movements meaning he was awakening. She had asked if he had family but Peter had shrugged, saying they weren't aware of any. She would ask her father to look, she thought, feeling a hand on her shoulder and then her father's voice praying for her and for Tierney before he walked away.

She looked around, feeling suddenly afraid, her eyes shooting to the window before she walked that way and stood, her eyes on the land around, lifting to the hills behind them. A shudder ran through her. Her mother was right. She had gone and done something, something she likely shouldn't have, and now her life was entwined with Tierney's and she had no idea who he was or where she went from there.

She turned as she heard a sound, eyes searching before they dropped to Tierney. She walked to the side of the bed, sitting, her hand reaching for his. At her touch, his movements stopped and his eyes flickered open, not quite focusing for a moment.

Tierney roused, a sense of safety surrounding him. He shuddered at the remembered beatings and threats, the deprivation he had undergone, and wondered. He could feel a softness under him and that couldn't be, he thought. Not the bunk he had had for the last couple of months.

He heard a soft voice talking to him and a soft hand on his, a woman's hand, he thought, and shuddered once more. Please, Lord, not that. Don't let a lady be his captive. His eyes opened and he blinked, not quite focusing. His eyes drifted shut and he lay there, trying to summon the energy to awaken once more. He listened to the soft voice, felt a gentle breeze, heard the songs of birds and insects, smelt the perfume of flowers, and wondered. He slept once more, feeling safe and comfortable.

Titus stood behind Larkin, before his hand rested on her shoulder.

"He was awake?"

"He roused, but not really awake. Is he going to make it, Uncle Titus?" Larkin looked up, hope on her face, something unreadable in her eyes.

"I think so, love. Now, your father's looking for you. Nothing bad. He just wants to talk with you." Titus nodded towards the door. "They have to head back late tonight. Go on. He won't bite."

"Funny, Uncle Titus." She reached to hug her uncle, her thanks whispered in his ear.

Liam walked towards his daughter as she stood on the back patio. Titus had told him what had happened, going into more detail that he normally would have. Liam was concerned, knowing that he didn't want his daughter facing what his sons had and having a feeling that was what was ahead of her.

Larkin watched her father, seeing the frown on his face, and sighing. Lord, please? I can't do this. I can't tell Dad what's going on when I don't even know myself and I just know he'll question me.

Liam swept his daughter into a hug and then stood her back, searching her face before he nodded, his arm around her shoulders turning her to a seating area.

"Sit, Larkin."

"Dad?"

"Ssh, Larkin. I'm not questioning you. I know you and the boys went in. And somehow I know that young man in there will thank you, at some point. Titus said he had to work hard to save him."

Larkin nodded. "It was horrible, Dad, where we found him. I had no idea people did that, not in this country."

"They can and do. We never know how much it goes on. Man's depravity and greed do that." He watched the flickering emotions on her face. "You're not happy, Larkin, and haven't been for months. Want to talk to your old worried father about that?"

She shook her head. "I can't, Dad, not because I don't want to. I just can't remember what happened to cause this." She looked at the clouds sailing across the blue sky. "Something did, and I just can't remember." She turned to look at him, a shuttered look coming over her face. "I know I have been difficult lately, and I'm sorry."

"We've talked about that, and you're forgiven. I'm just concerned, that's all."

"I know, Dad." She looked back at the house. "I think it has something to do with Tierney, and I don't know what."

"With Tierney? How? From what I understand, none of you have ever met him."

She nodded. "That's what we're told, but I think we have, Dad. At some point, our lives have crossed and I just don't know where or when."

He frowned as he studied her. "We have? I don't recognize the name. Titus has explained what he does but I don't remember him at all."

She nodded. "I know I have but I can't remember, and that's dangerous, Dad. What if I need to remember something to keep him safe, or I should have remembered something that would have prevented this?"

Liam's arm swept his daughter into a hug. "God would have used you to prevent this, if it had been His will. We don't know why Tierney went through what he did. We need to pray hard for him, sweetheart. He's going to need those prayers, to recover from his ordeal."

## Chapter 4

Rolling his head sideways, Tierney's eyes opened and he blinked, squinting against the low light that was on in the room. His head moved as he looked around, a frown covering his face for a moment. He didn't know where he was. All he knew was that it wasn't the cell he had been in for so long. How long, he just couldn't remember. He jumped as he felt a hand touch his face and his eyes slid closed. This was the hand he remembered, the hand that calmed him in his nightmares.

His eyes opened again and he searched, finding the woman, no, lady, sitting on the edge of the bed, her hand on his forehead, bringing comfort and calming. He couldn't understand what she was saying, and that perplexed him. He could see her lips moving and then he realized she was praying inaudibly. That brought a sense of peace.

His hand moved and he caught hers in his, bringing her eyes to him in first fright and then understanding. He tried to moisten his lips, wanting to speak, but unable to. He drank from the cup she held to his mouth, the effort almost too much, and he slipped back asleep.

Titus walked forward, his eyes on Tierney, watching closely.

"He was awake?"

Larkin nodded as she rose. "He was. He tried to speak, but couldn't. Uncle Titus, what are we to do?"

"What do you mean?"

"I mean. He's in danger still. We don't know who's after him or why. Peter spoke with the authorities. They found the building but there was no one there. It had been cleared out."

"That it had. That investigation is in their hands, Larkin, not ours. Our task is right here." He watched her. "But don't you have to go back to work?"

She shook her head. "No, I quit. I just didn't have a good feeling about that work, not anymore. I'll be needing to find something and soon."

"Stay here for now. I know you could go to your parents, but you don't want to. I don't know what you're searching for, Larkin, but you're not content and haven't been. Spend time with the Lord, my girl. That's what you need. And if you really need to work, I'll hire you to work around here. Lois will be needing surgery soon on that knee of hers and can use the help here until she recovers."

She looked at him, assessing his words, and then nodded. "I can do that, I think. Dad won't like it."

"It doesn't matter, Larkin. It's time you stood up for yourself. They have expected you to fit into a certain pattern all your life. Your whole family has done that. You've never rebelled and when you do speak up for yourself, you get beaten back down. They don't mean to do that, but that's what happens.

Your aunt and I would welcome you staying with us for now, if you want. And only if that's what you want." He pointed to Tierney. "I need your help with him. You're the only one who seems to be able to reach through the fog to him. If you leave, I don't have a clue what I'd do."

She nodded before she reached to hug him, turning as she heard movement from Tierney once more. Her uncle's hand stopped her and then turned her to the door.

"Go, love. Get yourself some rest. If he's waking, then we're going to have to watch closer for him."

A day later, Tierney stirred, his eyes opening and staying open. He searched for the lady, his princess, as he thought of her, but she wasn't there. An older man was, stooping to feel his wrist and then listening to his heart. He watched at the man pulled up a chair, writing something in a folder before he set it aside, his eyes assessing the younger man.

"Tierney, you're safe."

At the words, Tierney's eyes slid closed. He had been found. God heard after all. His eyes flew open and he searched the room.

"Where am I?" His voice was rough, the words barely audible.

"You're at my place. You were found and brought here. You gave us quite a scare, young man." Titus frowned as he watched Tierney searching. "You're looking for Larkin, I suspect. She's not here right now but she'll be back."

Tierney's eyes followed the movements of the man as he stood and then walked from the room. Exhausted, Tierney slept again, not waking until the early morning. He started, fear running through him. Early morning was when he was always pulled from his cell and the torture began. A hand on his stopped his movement and he looked down at the hand before his eyes raised to see Larkin sitting in the chair her uncle had left all those hours ago.

"You're awake. Oh, that's good." She reached to help him sip from a mug of water. "We were so worried." She didn't question him and he wondered at that.

"Thank you." His voice was still hoarse but a bit stronger than before. "Where am I?"

"You're safe. You're at my uncle's." She watched as he nodded.

"He told me. I forgot." He shoved at the blankets. "I need to leave. They'll find me. I don't want them to hurt you."

She shook her head. "They won't. They don't know who we were." She tilted her head, a frown on her face. "I know you, but I don't know where from."

He searched her face. "I know you, too, but from where?" He shook his head, his brow furrowed as he thought. "No, I don't know where from."

Larkin sighed. "I was hoping you would remember. Guess that scraps that idea."

He watched as she rose and began pacing, the frown deepening on his face. Yes, he knew her but he didn't know why. It was tickling at the back of his mind, the where and reason, but he just couldn't reach it.

A week later, ensconced on the couch, Tierney watched as Larkin paced once more, her arms wrapped around herself. He was worried about her and feared for her safety, but didn't know why.

"Larkin?" She turned as he spoke. "Larkin? Can you sit for a moment?"

She nodded, sliding down into a chair near him. "You have questions?"

"I do but they can wait. I'm still trying to decide where I know you from."

"It will come. Likely at the most inopportune moment." She studied him for a moment. "Are you really okay?"

He shook his head. "No. I'm not. I don't know that I ever will be." His face darkened at the remembered treatment he had undergone. "What I went through changes you." He looked up as he heard footsteps on the floor coming their way. He didn't recognize the young man standing in the doorway, the man's eyes on Larkin.

"Larkin?"

When the man spoke, Larkin's eyes slid closed and then her face went blank.

"Lincoln? What are you doing here?"

Lincoln Carmichael approached his sister, hugging her and dropping a kiss on her cheek before he sat on the couch, his eyes on her.

"I just came to see my sister. Can't I?"

She nodded. "Are you on your own or did Logan come to?"

He shook his head. "Logan didn't come. He doesn't know I'm here. I just wanted to see you and make sure you're okay."

"Well, I am." She snapped at him and then sighed. "I'm sorry, Lincoln. It's not your fault. I just need some time away from everyone." She was on her feet and running from the room. Tierney caught sight of the tears on her face before he turned to her brother.

"You made her cry."

Lincoln turned in astonishment at the accusation directed at him. "And?"

"You made her cry. Don't ever do that again."

"And just who are you to tell me that?" Lincoln, in his worry for his sister, was ready for a fight.

Tierney struggled to his feet, standing staring down at Lincoln. "Because she's too precious of a person to be put through that, by family or not." He turned and walked away, his steps slow and laboured at times.

Lincoln watched him and then his head went back as his eyes slid closed. That's not how I meant this to be, Lord. What happened?

Peter watched his cousin for a moment before he approached, dropping down onto the seat Tierney had walked away from.

"Lincoln, you need to back off from Larkin. She's hurting and doesn't want you to know."

---

"Hurting? How?" Lincoln watched his cousin closely.

"She's not saying. Dad's talked to her but she hasn't opened up to him." He pointed at the doorway. "And she's the only one who can calm Tierney down."

"She is?" Lincoln blew out a breath. "What's the story there, Peter, with Tierney?"

Peter shrugged. "We're working on that. But I can say that we were asked to go in and find him. For some reason, Larkin was asked to go. We don't know why and that is concerning."

"It is. I'm just so afraid for her."

"Tell her that and then let her make her own decisions. She's an adult but her brothers treat her as if she's still a child. That's what Tierney was saying, part of it."

Lincoln finally nodded. "You're right. We do. I need to find her to apologize."

"You won't find her, not today."

Lincoln stared at his cousin. "Why not?"

"Because she just drove away and that's concerning. She's in danger. Dad was just told that."

## Chapter 5

Walking through the town where her uncle lived, Larkin studied the businesses. She needed to find work, that she knew, but she really wasn't sure what she wanted to do anymore. Uncle Titus, you don't know how much I appreciate your offer of work, but I need to be independent. I can't continue living with you as much as you've made me welcome.

She sighed, reaching for her car keys, and heading back for her vehicle, not seeing the man following her, a camera raised to take her picture, before he turned and walked away. He had been successful, he thought. That was the woman they were looking for, whoever they were who had hired him. This finished off his work with them, he thought.

Larkin sat in her car, staring at her uncle's house, not sure what she wanted to do, and that was so unlike her. Lord, she prayed, I feel like I have something hanging over my head and I have no idea what or who. All I know is that I need to stay with Tierney, for some reason, and that I can't do. He'll be heading home to wherever it is he calls home soon. Uncle Titus said he should be able to be on his own in a couple of weeks, and I don't want him to go. Lord, please? Work on my attitude and show me where You want me. Heal Tierney. He is hurting so much, hurting in ways I can't even imagine.

Tierney turned from where he had been standing at the kitchen counter, a smile on his face as he saw Larkin. She stopped, then approached him, stopping again as she stood in front of him.

"Tierney, should you be up?"

He nodded. "I should. I need to do this, Larkin. Do you understand?"

"I do, unfortunately. Do you want something to eat?"

Tierney shook his head, his hand reaching for hers. "I just want to talk to you. Can we sit?"

She slid into a chair at the table, watching as he did likewise.

"Tierney? Have you remembered something?"

He shook his head. "No, and that's frustrating. Peter and James won't say who asked them to find me. Do you know?"

She shook her head. "No, and that's the thing of it. None of us know. I was specifically asked to go along. I have no experience in doing what we did." She paused, frowning, before her eyes found his. "It was just so strange. We walked in, found you, walked out and drove away. About thirty minutes later, our camper ran off the road and we had to run for safety. They didn't follow us. It's almost as if they knew where we were heading."

Tierney sighed as she said that. "It is more than likely that they did. That means everyone here is at risk."

Larkin studied the man in front of her, taking in the dark brown hair and curious shade of jade eyes with the brown flecks in them. "How do we protect ourselves then?"

He shrugged. "I don't know, Larkin. I just don't know." He reached for her hand, his thumb rubbing the back of it. "I'm sorry about your brother. I told him not to make you cry again."

"You did what?" She shook her head, disbelief on her face. "I bet that went over well. They don't get it. They smother me without realizing it." She bit at her lip. "I know Lincoln and Holly went through a bunch of stuff. He lost his memory and we didn't see him for a year. Logan and Aveleen had the same thing happen - an adventure they called it. Only hers took him away from us to Riverville, where she's from."

"Riverville? That's where I live. Or I did. I'm not sure if I'll stay there." He sighed. "I need to go to my place and soon. I think I have work I should have done."

"Let us take you then." She looked up as the door to the garage opened and her uncle walked in, followed by a tall younger man. "And here's the right person to do that." She rose and went to hug her uncle and then Murphy O'Brien, a friend of her brother's wife.

Tierney looked up, a frown turning to a smile. "Murphy? What are you doing here?"

"Looking for a friend. Good to see you, Tierney." Murphy shook Tierney's hand and then stood back, watching carefully as Larkin pointed to a chair and made Tierney sit again. He shared a look with Titus, who simply grinned.

Tierney looked at Larkin, a frown on his face, before he caught the look on Murphy's face. Murphy was watching Larkin closely with a concerned look on his face, and caught Tierney's movement as he turned his head. Murphy shook his head. Tierney knew they would talk later. This man did not show up just because, he thought. He was sent here.

Larkin finally rose, her eyes on the clock, and excused herself. She needed to change, she thought. I have to work on supper but I can't when the men are there. She returned to the kitchen a few minutes later to find the men had left. She could hear voices from her uncle's office and turned that way and then stopped, shaking her head. If and when they want me to know what's going on, they'll tell me, won't they, Lord? Right now, the task You've put in front of me is to provide a meal.

Murphy watched from the doorway before he approached Larkin, a hand on her arm stopping her as she turned from the stove. She looked up, a frown on her face.

"Murphy, please. I need to put this on the table."

He reached for the pan of meat, depositing it on the table and then pulled out a chair, seating her.

"Murphy? What is going on? Why are you here?" She began to shake, fear flowing through her. "You're scaring me."

"I'm sorry, Larkin. I didn't mean to." He sat, his hands reaching for hers. "I really didn't mean to. Adriel will have my head if I tell her I scared you." He paused, sorting through his thoughts, knowing he would scare her even more and not even sure yet why. A friend was still working through that. "Abe asked me to come. He had word that you're in danger and he wanted to make sure you were safe."

"How? What do you mean? I'm not the one who's in danger. That's Tierney." She watched as Murphy began to shake his head. "Murphy? What do you mean? No, it's not me. It's Tierney."

He could heard the panic starting in her voice and sighed. Lord, please help me to explain. I'm not even sure I understand.

"Emma got word that you're in danger. Someone said something to her over the past day or so. She's desperately running her programs, trying to find out who, but hasn't had any luck yet. I was sent to warn you. I also need to bring Tierney back to Riverville. Your uncle asked for that."

"He's leaving?" Her voice died away at the thought of not seeing him every day. "Murphy? How much danger is he in?"

"That we don't know about, Larkin. Abe, Gideon and Emma are working on that." Murphy had named his employer and his wife and Abe's brother-in-law, who was a private investigator. Abe ran a security company that trained security personnel. "I wish I knew better what you're facing."

She sighed. "When does he leave?"

"Tomorrow." Tierney dropped into a chair beside her. "I would like you to come to, Larkin, if you will. I could use a secretary."

She shifted in her chair to watch him, a closed look on her face. "And just why would you offer that, Tierney?"

"Because I remember how hard it was trying to do it all. Having been gone for so long, I'll have a lot to catch up on. I need someone to organize me and my work, and be a buffer. Could you do that?"

She shrugged, before she turned to Murphy, who was watching closely, a half smile on his face. Yes, Lord, they are attracted to one another, he thought, and here we go again.

"Murphy?" Larkin watched him, a frown on her face. "What aren't you saying?"

## Chapter 6

Watching through the vehicle window, Larkin studied the town they had just driven through. Riverville, she thought, not where I want to be. Not with Logan here. I won't have a life. She sighed. She had committed to working for Tierney but wasn't sure she should have. She felt a hand on hers and looked down. Tierney's hand covered hers and she wondered at the feeling of comfort, peace and safety that she felt. She knew the trip had been hard on him. She could see it in the whiteness of his face and the lines that had deepened.

Murphy pulled through a gate and passed a large house. Abe's, Larkin thought. What did I just go and do? Why did I ever agree to come here? Something's big is about to break loose and I want no part of it. She watched as Murphy stopped near a cabin, one right near Abe's large rambling home. She sighed again. Why, Lord? Why me?

Tierney roused, his eyes blinking open in the twilight, trying to remember where he was and unable to. The door opening beside him roused him a bit more and he nodded as Murphy spoke with him. He swung his legs out and tried to stand, unable to from fatigue and pain. Murphy's hands were there as were Matt's, the paramedic on Abe's team. A look was exchanged between the two men before they guided Tierney to the cabin and then to a bedroom.

Larkin hesitated, not sure where she should be and then following the men into the cabin, stopping in the kitchen, searching for a mug, cup, glass, whatever she could find for water for Tierney. She knew he needed that. She turned as she heard footsteps and saw Murphy watching her.

"Larkin?"

"What now, Murphy? You've pulled me here, set me behind a barricade and don't explain. You've brought me to a town my brother lives in. Didn't you get it that I was trying to get away from them? I need space. Now I won't have it." She spun, tears blinding her eyes and ran for the outdoors, not sure where she would end up, and just kept running, finally stopping at the edge of a lake.

Murphy sighed. "That went well, didn't it, Abe?" He turned to find his friend and business partner standing watching.

"We didn't think it would, did we? I know you tried to talk to her before you left. You said that but her whole focus is Tierney." Abe shot a look towards the bedroom, hearing soft voices as Matt spoke with Tierney. "You know, he's going to start remembering what happened."

"I know. That worries me, Abe. Larkin there is the only one who can calm him. And we can't let her stay with him all the time." "No, we can't." Murphy ran his hands through his hair and started for the door. "I need to go find her."

"Let me. You haven't had the latest update from Emma or Gideon." He stopped at the door. "Which way did she go?"

Murphy gave a bark of laughter. "Your guess is as good as mine. I would suspect a straight line and that leads to the lake." He groaned. "The lake and all that open area."

Abe gave a curt nod. "I know. If I don't find her, I'll call."

Larkin stood, arms wrapped around her, fear shaking her as it had never shaken her before. She turned in a circle, trying to see through the darkening evening but unable to. She sighed. That was stupid, wasn't it, Lord, to run like that and in a place I don't know? How do I find my way back?

She jumped as she heard a sound and a small scream escaped her.

"Who's there?" She hated the quaver of fear in her voice.

"It's okay, Larkin. It's Abe." He walked towards her, assessing her fear and her attitude. He sighed himself. She's running, Lord, and I have no idea why. This is not how this was to go.

"Abe?" She moved quickly towards him. "Is it Tierney?"

He shook his head, his hand coming out to gently take her arm and turn her towards the buildings. "No, Matt's still with him. He's okay as far as I know. It's you I'm worried about."

She stopped quickly, digging in her heels, not letting him move her forward. "Why does everyone keep saying that? Tierney's the one we went in and rescued. Not me."

"And that has everyone puzzled. He can't remember yet why he was taken, but he's afraid for you. He can't say why." Abe watched her as closely as he could in the dimness. "Someone is after you, Larkin. Emma had definite word on that tonight. Someone is looking for you. And when they do that, it's not usually in your best interests."

She shook her head, her hand going to her mouth. "Abe, why? I'm a secretary, or rather, I was. I didn't see anything I shouldn't have."

"That's what you may think but somewhere along the line, you have. That's what we're hearing." He walked her towards the lights. "For now, we need you to stay close to the house."

"Abe, I can't. I just can't. I can't be smothered." She swallowed hard, fighting back her fear and her tears. "Tierney? How is he?"

"I'll take you in to see him and then you're moving to our house." He held up a hand as she protested. "No, you can't stay in the cabin with him. It was different at your uncle's. Here, you two would be on your own and we can't have that. For tonight, Matt and Ian are taking turns with him. If he needs you, someone will come and find you."

Larkin paced the room she had been given, not yet ready to settle down for the night, but not ready to stay up either. She stopped at the window, pulling back the drape enough that she could watch the cabin where Tierney was housed. She had been allowed in to see him but he had been sleeping. She needed to talk to him, to hear him tell her it wasn't she that whoever it was wanted, but he hadn't been able to.

She finally sank down into a chair, her heart raised in prayer without being aware that was what she was doing. She slept at last, pulling a blanket

—

over her, not hearing the soft tap or the opening of the door as Emma, Abe's wife, peeked in and then quietly shut the door, shaking her head at Abe.

Early morning, she was awake and on her feet, running from the room and towards Tierney, knowing he needed her. She hit the outside door, flinging it open and heading for the bedroom, stopping in the doorway to watch.

Matt had roused earlier when he heard Tierney beginning to toss and turn. He had stood for a moment watching until Tierney's movements became more violent, his body twisting and turning, his head shaking from side to side, as he tried to articulate what he wanted to say, tried to avoid the remembered blows he had taken. Matt strode to the bed, his hands out to try and stop the movements before he stood back, shock for a moment on his face as he listened.

Tierney was reliving days of torture, days of being asked where Larkin was, where he knew her from. He shook his head, his words mumbling as he spoke. He denied that he knew her, that he could find her. He refused to help them, stating he would never bring her to them, no matter what they did to him. His words turned to shouts and then to sobs as he refused, finally turning to whispers. His body moved the whole time.

Ian was there and with Matt, tried to calm him, to hold him still, their voices telling him he was safe, but he still fought them, trying to get up and away, his voice calling for Larkin.

Larkin was at his side, dropping to her knees, as she heard him calling for her, her hand reaching for his that he had flung over his head, her other hand on

40

his forehead, her voice low and calming. His head turned as his eyes opened, searching for her, finding her.

"You're here. You're safe. Thank God. They wanted me to bring you to them. I can't. Larkin, you need to hide. They'll find you." His voice died away as he calmed and finally slept.

Larkin stayed on her knees, afraid to move, afraid to take her hands away, knowing if she did, he would rouse and the nightmares would return. She felt Matt's hands on her arms, raising her to her feet and then gently pushing her down into a chair.

Matt and Ian moved to the doorway, Matt turned so he could watch the couple.

"Matt?" Ian's voice was hushed.

Matt shook his head, his eyes on Larkin. "I've heard of this, Ian, but never seen it. How did she know to come? We didn't go for her."

"I know. That's spooky, the way she just showed up." Ian looked towards the door as it quietly closed. "Abe?"

"Emma said she heard Larkin running through the house. What happened?"

"We couldn't get Tierney awake from his nightmare. She just appeared and quieted him." Matt nodded towards the kitchen. "We need to talk, Abe."

Abe took the mug of coffee handed him and leaned against the counter, his eyes on the kitchen doorway. "Okay. What's going on?"

"We know why Tierney was taken, not just by who." Matt and Ian exchanged a grim look. "He was taken to get to Larkin. He was talking tonight, reliving what happened. It sounds as if they were trying to get him to find Larkin and bring her to whoever it was."

Abe nodded. "That's what we're hearing. But who is behind it? That's what we're having trouble finding out."

"And just who would be after me? You keep saying that, but you can't tell me who." Larkin stood in the doorway, a frown on her face as she searched the men's faces. "And don't tell me not to worry. I can't not do that."

Abe nodded even as he pointed at a chair. "Larkin, please. Sit. I need to talk to you. I just wasn't expecting it to be this early." He squinted at the clock and groaned. "It's only four in the morning."

"It is. Every day, Tierney awakes at three and we have a fight on our hands to calm him down. That's the time of day he was awakened for over two months, taken to a room, questioned, and tortured. Did you even know that?" She looked around, shaking her head. "Of course, you didn't. You weren't there every morning, just like Uncle Titus, the boys and I. Even Aunt Lois had her turn with Tierney." She dropped her head, fatigue weighing her down for a moment, before she looked up. "What he said today? That is mild to what I've heard. I've heard the fear and yes, terror in his voice as he calls for me. How can I stay away from him?"

## Chapter 7

Tierney paused as he heard Larkin's voice, catching the sobs in it, knowing she had been hearing his mumblings and ramblings. His heart broke for her, and he wanted to take back his words, only that wasn't possible. He stood behind her for a moment before he reached to encircle her with his arms, feeling her jump and then relax back against him.

"Larkin, I'm so sorry. I didn't know you had heard." His voice was soft in her ear, quiet enough that she was the only one who heard him.

"I did. Tierney, you shouldn't be up." She twisted in his arms, reaching to try and push him back towards his bedroom.

His hands came up to stop her. "Larkin, Abe needs to talk to you. He's not here for his health, but yours." He turned her and made her sit, nodding at Abe as he dropped into a chair beside her, reaching for her hand as he did so.

Abe nodded, his eyes on Larkin, knowing what he would have to say would not be taken well. He would not be speaking lightly, he knew, not with what Emma had told him. He had had a long discussion with the police chief in town, Caleb Logan, and had processed what his suggestions had been.

"Larkin?" When she refused to look at him, his face grew stern. "Larkin, look at me. Larkin!" His voice had a bite to it that made her jump and glare at him. "Larkin, your very life and the lives of those around you will depend on you responding to us the first time we speak to you. Do you understand that?"

She shook her head. "No, actually, I don't. I hear whispers and comments but no one has ever said what the danger is, who it's from, or why."

Tierney tightened his hand on Larkin's even as his arm came around her. "I think that's what Abe wants to tell you. You need to listen to him, please."

Larkin turned to face him, her eyes searching his, seeing something there that made her frown but gave her hope. She nodded. "I can do that. I just don't want smothered. I've had enough of that."

Murphy had to rub his upper lip to control his grin, seeing Ian grinning at her and Abe shaking his head.

"We'll try not to smother you, Larkin, but we are concerned. We don't like it when the ladies in our lives are threatened." Abe looked down for a moment before he looked up at her again. "This is where we stand. Just let me speak and then we'll try and answers what questions we can."

She nodded. "Okay, I guess that's what we do."

Abe looked down again, trying to control his smile, not quite successful. Tierney, he thought, you have a handful there, more so than I think you realize.

"This is it, Larkin. You are in grave danger, whether you realize it or not. This thing with Tierney? For some reason, you have been connected to him. The whole thing with him? It was to make him bring you to whoever it is. The word we have received is that you saw something you shouldn't have and it involved Tierney as well, but you're the one they are after. We're working on that, but we can't figure out what it is. Only you can tell us that.

"Tierney has been adamant that he has never met you, has never met your family, other than Logan at church. What he went through was brutal. And you know that. What we need to determine is who and why." Abe was not telling her everything, that the threats had been escalating every day. Tierney was aware of it, he had asked directly before leaving Titus' home.

Larkin stared at him before her head began to shake. "That can't be. I don't remember ever seeing Tierney before." She turned to look at him. "At least, I don't think I ever did."

"I don't think you have, not directly." Abe's words brought her eyes back to him. "It may be something you saw him doing, somewhere you saw him, someone you saw him with. If it was a fleeting moment, you might not ever remember."

"And I need to. I need to so Tierney is safe." She was more concerned about him than her own safety. "But how do I do that?"

"That's what we need to work on. No, we won't smother you. That's a given. Until we know for sure who it is and why, we can't make plans. You two need to live your normal lives." He stopped as Larkin yawned and then rose.

---

"I'm sorry, Abe. I can't do this right now." Her feet stumbled as she walked towards the door before she righted herself and disappeared.

Ian had risen to follow her and was back in a few minutes. "She's in the house, Abe. Emma was there."

Abe nodded, even as his eyes went to Tierney before he rose and hauled Tierney to his feet and directed him back to his bed. He shook his head. This has gotten us nowhere, has it, Lord? I guess it's in Your hands.

Tierney was on a search a day later. Abe had spoken with him again, letting him know they were no further ahead. Tierney had nodded and then informed Abe he was moving home, he had to. He had work waiting and needed to get to that. When Abe questioned him about Larkin, he had just shrugged and walked away.

Larkin looked up from the flowers she had been looking at, her hand falling away from them as she studied Tierney's face. She didn't want him to walk away from her, ever. Nor did she want to walk away from him, but would if it meant keeping him safe.

"Larkin, can we talk?" Tierney reached for her hand, drawing her down on a nearby bench.

Larkin waited, not sure what Tierney was up to.

"I'm moving home tomorrow, Larkin. I need to."

She nodded. "I suspected that you would. But what happens when you have a nightmare? Who calms you then?"

Tierney sighed. She had gone right to the heart of the matter. "I have no idea. I pray that I don't have them, but I know I will." He paused, wanting to ask a question, but not sure how she would take it. "I do want you to come work for me."

She studied him. "If you're sure. You know nothing about my employment history."

"I don't need to. I know you." He looked around, not seeing anyone close to them. "How come you've never married?"

She stared at him before she laughed. "Dad. Lincoln. Logan. Does that say it all?"

"What do you mean?"

"I mean, I have never had a boyfriend. I have had ones want to go out with me but they look at those three and walk away. They don't realize what they have done. And I can't talk to them. They don't listen to me."

Tierney's arm had come around her at that point and he hugged her to him, sorrow that she had had to face this, but gladness in his heart as he could then ask a question he still wasn't sure he should.

"I can see that." He bit at his lip before he spoke. "I am going to ask a question and I'm not sure I even should." She had shifted so she could watch him. "Larkin, you're in grave danger. I'm part of it. What I would like to ask, is will you partner with me for the duration? Will you consider marrying me, just until we get through this?"

She shook her head, shock on her face. "Tierney! Why?"

"Because you are a very beautiful, funny, loving, compassionate lady I would like to help keep safe. I treasure your friendship. I treasure you as the person you are."

She continued to stare at him. "Tierney, are you really asking me to marry you? Because if you're not, I don't consider this a very nice joke." She struggled to get away but his arms tightened on her.

"I am, Larkin. Trust me when I say this is not something I am asking lightly." He sighed and removed his arm from around her. "You don't deserve a proposal like this. You need to be courted, to have flowers and gifts brought to you, to be taken out for romantic dinners, walks, whatever it is you would like to do." He rose, staring at the ground, before he looked at her, shook his head, and walked away.

Larkin sat, her hand to her mouth, shock on her face. Tierney really did mean it, didn't he? Oh, Lord, what do I do? How do I go around him now? She rose herself, heading for the house, not seeing anyone around her and she was glad. She needed to be by herself. She paced her bedroom, finally heading to find Emma.

"Emma, do you know if there are any apartments for rent in town?"

Emma turned, a question on her face. "There are, but you're welcome to stay here."

Larkin shook her head. "No, I need to move to town. I don't have transportation. Besides, I don't want to be around your little one, not when I'm in danger."

Emma studied her for a moment and then nodded. "I know of a couple that are for rent. Friends of mine have some buildings." She looked at the clock and reached for Larkin's hand. "Come on. We can go now."

"Emma! We can't just walk in on them."

"We can. I know the apartments are empty and they would like to rent them. One is over a bakeshop."

"A bakeshop? The Irish one?"

Emma nodded. "It is. Dave and Rylee really want to rent it but they're choosy. You would suit them fine."

"I can't. Much as I would love living above a bakeshop, I can't bring danger to them." She looked in astonishment as Emma began to laugh.

"Trust me, you being in danger won't be an issue. I'll let them tell you their story, but Rylee was kidnapped at one point and then left in a crawlspace to die."

"What! Emma! Don't tell me that."

## Chapter 8

Two hours later, Larkin stared down at the keys in her hand, knowing she had made the right move but still worried about bringing danger to her new friends. Rylee and Dave had both assured her they weren't concerned at all. Emma had hugged her, asked her if she needed help bringing her belongings from her home town, and volunteered the guys to do just that. Larkin had just shook her head, handed Emma the keys to the storage unit she had her belongings in and asked if they would clear it out for her.

Emma had looked at the keys and then at Larkin with a look in her eyes.

"Are you sure?"

"I am, Emma. I need to do this. Mom and Dad don't know yet that I had given up my apartment three weeks ago. I did it before this all started with Tierney. I just can't continue to live there and I don't know why. Something scared me too much for that to happen."

"What scared you, Larkin?"

Larkin had shrugged, not willing to admit that she had felt followed and that she had been receiving threats. That was too personal.

"Larkin? Were you threatened?" Emma went right to the heart of the matter before she hugged Larkin. "We're in good company then. Someday, all

50

the guys will tell you their stories. They had adventures as they call it with their ladies."

Larkin looked at her, her mouth opening and closing before she found her all. "All of them?" When Emma nodded, she continued. "You and Abe, too? Who else?"

Emma laughed as she drove back towards home. "Let's see. Dave and Rylee, Doug and his Darcy, and six other friends."

Larkin shook her head. "There is no way that happened. It was bad enough that my brothers did." She studied her new friend. "Emma, thank you for today. I don't know what's going to happen. I worry about Tierney on his own when he has these nightmares."

"What I suggest is that if you can, call him before three each morning, just to wake him up and maybe prevent them. If not, he'll make it through them." She paused. "I know. We'll find him a dog. He doesn't have one, does he?"

Larkin snapped her mouth closed. "I don't think so. Do you have a dog in mind?"

Emma nodded, turning down a side street and heading away from home. "I do. A friend has some she's ready to re-home."

Larkin watched as the Sheltie pups ran around the yard at Emma's friend, Laycee's home. She had fallen in love with a little bi-blue one but she knew she couldn't take it. Laycee and Emma had watched her and Laycee nodded at Emma. This one would stay with her for now, until Larkin was ready.

"Which one, Larkin?"

Larkin looked up at Laycee. "I don't know, Laycee. I'm not sure about this. I need to talk to Tierney first. This is something he needs to make a decision on."

"Then, talk to him and bring him here."

Tierney looked up as he felt the swing he was seated on move and Larkin sat beside him, her arms wrapped around herself.

"I was looking for you a while ago."

Larkin nodded. "Emma took me into town. I have an apartment there now. I'm moving tomorrow too." She sighed. "I just won't have my stuff yet."

"Don't you have to close your apartment or house or whatever you were living in?"

She shook her head. "I had already done that. I quit my job and was moving. I just hadn't told my family." She sighed. "I felt someone watching me and felt threatened. I thought if I moved suddenly, I would lose them. Guess that didn't work."

"What do you mean?" Tierney was beginning to worry.

"I felt someone watching us today when we were in town. I couldn't see anyone."

Tierney paused before he spoke. "How long have you felt like this?"

She shrugged. "Months. It started when Lincoln wouldn't contact us." She sighed, a bleak look coming across her face, even as she blinked back tears. "I couldn't say anything. They were too worried about Lincoln."

"And you didn't think they wouldn't worry about you as much?" Tierney tugged her closer into a hug. "They would have."

"But I couldn't tell them. I had no idea who it was. I talked to a friend and he looked into it for me but told me it likely wouldn't go anywhere, not without some idea of who." She sighed again. "I thought moving away would help."

"No, it hasn't, has it?" He laid his chin on the top of her head. "We need to talk to Abe."

She shook her head, struggling to get away from him, even as he tightened his hold on her.

"No, I can't. I won't, Tierney." She had not seen Abe standing near them, having come to find them.

"Larkin?" Abe's voice cut through her panic and she sighed.

"You heard."

"I did. I wasn't meaning to eavesdrop." He dropped down into a chair, his eyes on Larkin's face or what he could see of it. "What else, Larkin? And does Emma know how you felt today?"

Larkin shook her head. "I didn't tell her. I wasn't sure if I really did feel that or if it was everything just culminating. As to my old town, that's in the past."

"No, Larkin. It's not. Something there triggered all this with Tierney." Abe paused, his eyes going to Tierney. "Tierney, were you ever in her hometown, Hope, is it?"

---

Tierney went to shake his head and then his eyes slid closed. "I was. About the time her brother was away. I went there to meet someone about a document. Only he never showed. I talked to someone else though. He didn't give a name and only wanted general information." Tierney pulled out his phone and scrolled through his contacts. "He gave me a name and phone number and I saved it. I doubt it's going to be much good though."

"Let me have it and I'll pass it on to Emma or Gideon. They'll research it." Abe handed Tierney back his phone. "Now, as to what we do with you two."

"Tierney's moving home. And I found a dog for him. And I'm moving into an apartment. Emma found it for me." Larkin was on her feet and running for the house, unable to control her emotions and not wanting Tierney to see her in tears once more.

Tierney had stood, watching, before he slumped back into his seat, turning to Abe.

"How do we do this, Abe? How do we keep her safe when she runs from us?"

"It's hard, Tierney. I understand from what you've said that she has felt smothered all the time. She's rebelling, taking a stand, making noise. She just doesn't understand how unsafe it is for her."

"She understands, Abe, more than you think. At this point, she really doesn't care. She just wants her freedom." He sighed. "I have no idea how her family will take it." He stopped talking, spinning to stare at the house. "What was that she said about a dog?"

---

Abe started to laugh. "She didn't tell you? Emma took her to a friend's place, stating you needed a dog if you were going to live on your own. Just for company and comfort and to help you through your nightmares. Larkin refused to make a choice for you, although I understand she fell in love with one."

"Get it for her."

"We can't, Tierney, just for the same reason she refused to get you one. You have to make that decision and so does she." Abe studied the younger man. "If you need to talk to someone and I'm sure you do, I can give you a name or two."

Tierney nodded. "I think I do."

"Then, talk to Greg, our minister. He was in the forces as a chaplain. And Doug's Darcy. She's a psychologist, forensics one, but she called me today, asking if you were seeing anyone and for you to call her."

"She did that?"

"She did. She considers you a friend, did you know?"

## Chapter 9

Larkin wandered her new home, fussing with her furniture. Emma had been as good as her word, sending some of Abe's men to Hope to bring back Larkin's belongings. She has asked if Larkin had wanted to go but Larkin had refused. She knew she had to talk to her parents but had sent an email, letting them know she had a new job in a new town and that she'd be in touch. She just knew Logan and Lincoln would track her down and try to move her back home. How she could avoid that, she still didn't know. She turned as she heard the doorbell, moving to study the video showing who was there. Dave had told her they installed a camera doorbell for her and that she could see who was there before she opened the door. She had thanked him, not quite sure she wanted that, but now she was glad.

Tierney walked up the stairs behind Larkin, watching her closely. Things were changing now, and he knew he didn't like it. He didn't like it that she was on her own and that he couldn't see her as often as he had.

Larkin turned, catching a look on his face, pausing before she spoke.

"You're sure you have work for me?"

He grinned. "I do. I looked over the mail and all that yesterday. It will take days to go through it. And I have requests to look at manuscripts that I need to go over." He sighed. "And I just don't feel like doing that."

"We'll organize the mail in the morning and then go from there. It's not likely as bad as you thought." She looked up. "What about the bills?"

"My accountant looked after that. She comes in every week and gets the bills and pays them. That's an agreement we've had for years. It's just all the other stuff we need to look at."

"And I imagine about half is likely junk mail or solicitation."

He nodded, before he looked around her living room. "This is nice. Dave and Rylee did a nice job on this apartment. They tore it all the way to the outside wall and redid it."

"And they don't ask enough for rent." She sounded down and she knew it. She sighed. "Sorry. That's not quite how I meant it."

"No, they don't charge enough." He took the mug of coffee she offered him. "Now, where do we go, Larkin?"

She shrugged, not looking at him. "I don't know, Tierney. Really, I don't. With this hanging over my head and you recovering, we shouldn't be making any decisions."

He looked at her, a glint of mischief in his eyes. "What's this I hear about a dog?"

She groaned. "Did Emma tell you?"

"No. She told Abe and Abe told me. I think it's a good idea, but you need one too."

She shook her head. "No, I don't think so. Dogs and I don't mix."

"You're sure on that?"

---

She nodded. "I don't want any pets, not right now." She looked up at him. "You understand, don't you?"

"I do. Now, about these threats. We need to look into them."

She shook her head. "I can't let anyone be hurt because of me."

"It's too late for that, Larkin. Someone already has been."

She looked away before looking back. "You mean yourself."

He shook his head. "No, not that. I mean you. You've been hurt and have covered it up. Please, never do that with me. Let me know if you get more or if you feel watched. I want to know. We also need to let Abe know."

"Right, we'll just do that. Then, he moves in and smothers me."

"He won't. Not unless he needs to. And he will talk to you first. He's promised me that."

"He did?" When Tierney nodded, she turned away, trying to cover her emotions. She jumped as she felt his arms come around her.

"What we talked about and what I asked? Just think on it. That's all I ask." He felt her nod and then stepped back. "I won't push you, Larkin. I've said my piece."

She turned, studying him. "I know you have. I just need to think about it and pray about it. It's not how I expected to receive a proposal."

"No, it's not, and I shouldn't have." He turned towards the stairs. "I'll pick you up in the morning. Come and lock up after me."

She trudged back up the stairs, her mind awhirl with emotions. This was not how she had planned her life. Who changed the direction of it, she wondered, and then sighed. I know, Lord, I know. It was You. But did it have to be so drastic?

She didn't see the man standing watching the lights go out in the apartment. He had turned in the photos he had taken but they had asked for more. It was only a fluke that he had found her. Somehow he knew that if he hadn't, it would not have gone well.

Larkin turned in a circle the next morning, studying Tierney's office, and then nodded. He had set up another desk for her, providing everything she would need for work. She didn't think she had ever had all she needed to do a task.

Tierney looked up from the mail he was sorting, a smile on his face as he watched her. This is the right decision for now, isn't it, Lord? She's here with me and I can watch for her. Then, he sighed, knowing he wasn't yet back to his full strength. That he had been told would still be a while. The nightmares continued to plague him and he wanted them over.

"Larkin?"

She looked around as he spoke and then moved towards him, her hands reaching for the piles of mail. "Let me. You get busy with your manuscripts. I'll sort this and then come find you." She turned to her desk and sat, her eyes on the mail, a frown on her face. She still wasn't sure she had made the right move, but God hadn't stopped her, not yet, anyway.

Her hand froze as she reached for the plain white envelopes, and there were more than one. She counted. A dozen of them, she thought. Almost as many as the number of weeks Tierney had been away. She turned as she heard his footsteps approaching.

"Larkin? What happened?" He reached for an envelope until her hand on his stopped him.

"We need to bring in the police, Tierney. These have been sitting here now for weeks." She looked up at him, fear briefly flickering on her face before she schooled her features to a neutral look.

He sighed. "You're right. Set them aside for now until someone comes." He turned away from her to reach for his phone, fighting the dizziness that hit every once in a while.

Frankie Brennan, a detective with the Riverville force, stood there, his eyes assessing Larkin as she spoke with him. He looked over at Tierney, who he knew somewhat from the young adults group at church and sighed. Here we go again, don't we, Lord. Friends and their adventures. This is getting old.

"These are all of them?" Frankie's voice was quiet as he spoke, his mind already racing with the possibilities of what the envelopes held.

"So far. The mail hasn't come yet today, I don't think, has it, Tierney?" Larkin spun in her chair to look for Tierney, finding him returning with a handful of mail.

Frankie reached for it. "If I may?" He quickly looked through the mail, not finding another envelope. He picked up one of the ones Larkin had set aside. "These didn't come through the regular mail. No stamps on them."

"So someone just walked up to the door, deposited them into the mailbox and walked away. Is that what you're saying?" Tierney was frustrated. "So, who? They've sat for weeks now. Was it the ones who held me captive or another party?"

Frankie groaned. "You just had to go and say that, didn't you?"

Tierney shrugged. "It makes sense, you know. Why would Party A be sending letters to my home, knowing I wasn't there?"

Frankie stared at him, a thought crossing his mind. "Where did you disappear from?"

Tierney looked up, a frown on his face. "From Hope. I was there to meet someone, only I can't remember who." He spun, almost running for his desk, and sat, bringing up his calendar and searching back. "Here. This is the name and the contact number of the person." He frowned again. "Only, I don't think he was there. I don't remember meeting anyone. I think I was there, he didn't show, and I went to leave. I don't remember much after leaving the restaurant we were to meet at."

Frankie nodded. "Your car was found abandoned along the side of the road. Smitty's brought it back for you at Caleb's request. We searched it and searched along the roads and surrounding area. You had just disappeared. There were no signs of a struggle, which was strange."

Tierney stared at him before he heard Larkin's soft intake of breath.

"He was drugged? Is that what you're saying?" Larkin went right to the heart of Frankie's observation.

"That's likely a good possibility. With the name of the restaurant, we can now go back and see if anyone remembers anything. Not likely, though, after all this time." He gathered up the evidence bags he had used and walked away, leaving Tierney and Larkin staring at one another.

## Chapter 10

A week later, Larkin stood from her desk and stretched. As she had promised Tierney, it had not taken that long to get him organized again. He had had to leave for the day, promising to be back before she left. She squinted at the large grandfather clock and sighed. He wasn't back and it was time for her to leave. She had no transportation and that worried her. She didn't feel safe walking all that way on her own.

A sound startled her and she spun, seeking the direction it came from. When it came again, she ran, looking for a hiding place, tucking herself in beside a cupboard and waiting. She heard the soft footsteps and the sounds of someone searching before silence came again.

Tierney paused, keys in hand, as he stared at the open front door, his heart in his mouth. He ran for the door, sliding to a halt on the polished dark hardwood of the hall, searching for Larkin.

"Larkin?" When she didn't answer, he ran for the office, calling for her again. "Larkin? Are you here?"

He spun as he heard a sound and caught her to himself as she launched herself from her hiding place. His arms tightened on her as she shook before she shoved away from him.

"Someone came in, Tierney. The door was locked and they still came in. I hid but they were looking for something or for one of us." Larkin's face showed the fear she was trying hard to hide. "You just missed them."

"I know. The door was open. That's strange." Arm around her, he walked her outside and tucked her into his car. "Sit here. I'll have to call it in."

Frankie stood back and watched Tierney pacing by the car, Larkin watching the activity around the house, before he approached them.

"Tierney?"

Tierney spun at the voice speaking to him and then relaxed.

"Frankie? Someone broke in while Larkin was on her own. She hid but I don't like it."

Frankie shook his head. "She did good, hiding, but who would break in? Don't you have a security system?"

"I do, but the lines were cut. Even the wireless backup didn't work." He frowned. "That's really strange. It should have."

"We'll look into it. In the meanwhile, have Abe's men set up a new one for you." He nodded at the car. "How's Larkin?"

"Scared. Mad. Hurt. What would you expect her to be like?" Tierney's voice had a bite and an edge to it that Frankie hadn't heard from him before. "This has to stop, Frankie. I can't have her scared like this."

Frankie dipped his head to watch Larkin again, a frown on his face. "Did she see anything?"

"No. She said she heard a noise and ran and hid. I had to hunt for her when I came in." He paused. "She said I just missed whoever it was."

Frankie's face grew stern at that. "They're watching you two very closely, aren't they? It's Friday night, end of the work day. You two could have disappeared and no one would have been the wiser." He turned as he heard Larkin's indrawn breath. "Larkin?"

"Is that what was planned?"

Frankie shrugged. "It's a possibility. Look, I need you to go somewhere for a while. The team will likely be a bit yet."

Larkin stared at him before she spun and walked away, her strides rapid. Tierney stared after her before he moved to his car and headed out. Frankie watched, shaking his head. You have a live one there, Tierney. And you have your hands full.

Tierney pulled to a stop beside Larkin and then approached her on foot as she stood, her eyes fixed ahead of her.

"Larkin?"

"Tierney, when does it stop? When are we safe?" She turned her head and he saw the traces of tears on her face. "I don't cry like this, Tierney. I never have, not in my whole life."

He reached to hug her and then turned her back to his car, shutting the door behind her and then walking around to slide in himself. He didn't drive away, just sat, his eyes on the road ahead of him, his fingers tapping against the wheel, that was, until

Larkin's hand reached out and stilled them. He turned his head, watching her closely.

"What do we do, Tierney? I have this bad feeling that this is only starting for us. I don't want you to go through anything more on my behalf."

"Somehow, Larkin, I don't think they really care about that. They're after you and that's all that concerns them. As to what we do, I don't know." He groaned as his phone rang and he pulled it out. "It's Caleb." He dropped the phone into the console.

"You need to answer that."

He shook his head. "Caleb will catch up with me later, I'm sure. Right now, you're what matters." As she went to protest, his fingers covered her lips. He sighed. "Larkin, I didn't know you before, but you've become important to me. Please, don't belittle yourself. I know what you're going to say."

Anger flared briefly in her eyes and then she relaxed. "You're right. I was going to say I wasn't worth it." She looked out the side window, not seeing the frown and then the look of hurt that crossed his face.

"Who beat you down so far?"

She spun, her hair flying around her face enough that she had to grasp it with her hands. "What do you mean?"

"What I said. You've been beaten down, not realizing your worth." He refused to back down from his comments and refused to look away.

Her eyes slid closed. "I let them do that to me."

"Let who?"

"Dad, Lincoln, Logan. I let them beat me down. They don't know they did that. I mean, they love me and all, but they're so protective, I feel like I have no life."

"And then I go and ask you to marry me, a complete stranger." He drew a deep breath, ready to speak, when she spoke.

"Tierney, no, you didn't do that. You build me up. You make me feel special, that I am a person of value, someone whose ideas and thoughts are important enough to you that you listen. You let me be me." She groaned. "Did I really just say that?"

He grinned. "You did and you can't take it back." Then he sobered. "I don't think they realize just how they've protected you. I'm surprised your Dad or Lincoln haven't shown up yet."

She looked out the side window. "Yeah, well, there's that too."

His hand reached for hers. "You haven't told them, have you? And you've been avoiding Logan?" At her nod, he smiled. "You can't avoid them forever, you know."

"I know. I just want to until whatever this is has completed, is finished, whatever."

He grinned again, his hand reaching for her cheek. "I meant what I said, Larkin. I will marry you, if you'll have me."

She studied him before she sighed. "You're doing it again, you know."

He just grinned at her and then pulled away from the side of the road, frowning as a car followed

---

67

him. He drove through Riverville and then spun the wheel to head down a residential street. Larkin stared at him and then through the back window.

"What is going on?"

"We have a tail, I think." He looked. "I think I lost him, but he likely knows where you live."

She shook her head. "You're such a bundle of good news, aren't you?" She stared out the window for a moment. "Tierney, can you find somewhere we can have a meal and then talk?"

"I can. Do you want to go to Mac's?"

"The cafe?" She shrugged. "Sure. Why not. Isn't that where everyone always ends up?"

He paused at the intersection and then turned away from there. "No, I think we need to go somewhere special. Just for you." He parked near an Italian restaurant and came around to open her door, his hand taking hers and not letting go. "This is a nice restaurant. Just what we want."

She studied it and then him, a slight frown on her face before she gave a small smile. "You're making this hard, you do realize that?"

"I'm not meaning to. I just thought you deserved a fancier place."

## Chapter 11

His eyes on Larkin, Tierney was puzzled. He just couldn't read her tonight, he thought. Whatever is going on, she's hidden it from me. I wish she wouldn't.

Their meal over and their dessert in front of them, Larkin looked up, her eyes searching Tierney's face, and then she nodded.

"Tierney?" She paused, her words dying on her lips, as she looked down, not sure how to proceed.

"Larkin? It's okay. You're going to say no, aren't you?"

She looked up, shaking her head. "No, that's not what I wanted to say. I think I would say yes, but it's not fair to you. You need to find a lady to love, who will cherish the man you are and love you back."

"And who's to say you're not her?" He smiled, his hands reaching for hers. "We need to really talk this through, do we?"

She shook her head again. "No. I've prayed about it and God has not said no. I know why you're doing this, I think, at least part of it. I'm just afraid I'll put you into more danger."

"Not likely. We're in this together." He dropped money on the table and then reached to draw her to her feet. "Let's walk. There's a park near here we can find a bench and talk."

After seating her on his favourite bench in the park, he watched as she struggled to find the words she needed and waited. He would not rush her, he thought.

"Tierney, I am saying yes." She turned to him. "God help me, I'm saying yes. I just know that you'll be in more danger."

His arm around her drawing her to him, he shrugged. "God is in control, and He will help us." He sat for a few moments. "We'll need to make plans."

She shook her head. "Can't we just go and do it? If we make plans, I won't have a say."

He stared at her. "What do you mean? Don't you want all the frills and whatever?"

"No, I don't. If I tell Mom, she'll pick out my dress, decide a meal, and just go to town on all the decorations and invitations. I don't want that. I want simple. She'll be complicated and fussy. Dad will put you through the third degree and then walk around frowning the whole time. The boys will challenge you and likely try and prevent it." She looked at him. "Can't we just go and do this?"

"I don't want you to regret anything, my love. Are you sure?"

She nodded. "I am. I always said I wanted to get married in my blue jeans. But I guess that doesn't work so well." She sighed as she felt her phone vibrate and pulled it out. "It's Mom. I need to talk to her but what do I say?"

"You don't have to say anything yet. We haven't finalized our plans. That's something we need to work on." He shook his head as she stuck her phone away. "You can't avoid her forever, you know. They likely know you've moved."

"They do. I sent them an email, but didn't tell them exactly where in Riverville I was living." She looked at the sky, seeing the darkening of the night. "We need to go, Tierney. You need to get back to your place."

"Not until we sort out something." She turned to look at him. "No matter what happens, Larkin, I will do my best to keep you safe. That I promise. Now, I guess we need to go talk to Greg."

She sighed. "I know we do. I'm not looking forward to that."

He was puzzled. "Why not?"

"Because the last couple of ministers we've had, every time I did something on my own, he ran to my parents or my brothers. I can't handle that anymore."

He pulled her to her feet, her hand tight in his. "Greg's not like that, my love. He keeps a confidence. That I know for a fact."

She sighed. "I'm sorry, Tierney. This has just been too much." She stumbled as she walked, fatigue setting in.

He walked her to her door, waited until she locked up and then stood, his hand against it, his head bowed in prayer. Lord, I have no idea why she said yes. I'm not sure she does. Please, dear Lord, let this be the right decision. I know I love this lady already, but I'm not able to tell her that. Not yet.

———

He turned and walked away, lost in thought, not seeing the man watching him, glancing at the lights in Larkin's apartment before he shoved away from the wall and followed Tierney.

Tierney took the house keys the officer handed him with a word of thanks. He paused in the hallway, not sure why he was afraid, but he suddenly was. And even more afraid for Larkin. He walked through the house, searching, knowing something was off but not sure what.

He paused in the office, knowing something was wrong in there, and walked towards his desk, pausing as he stared down at it. A sigh was drawn from him. They wouldn't have known, he thought, reaching for his phone.

"Frankie? Are you home or at work?"

"I'm just heading home but I can swing by. Why?"

"Because I have an envelope on my desk that shouldn't be here. Sorry to wreck your evening."

Frankie studied the envelope, latex gloves on his hands, before he opened it, his eyes raising to Tierney.

"You hadn't opened it?"

He shook his head. "No. I just got home. Why?"

Frankie turned the photo so Tierney could see it. Tierney's breath drew in sharply.

"That's tonight. How did it get in here with an officer here?"

"That's what I want to know. They're closer to you two than I realized." Frankie turned to walk away and then spun back. "We'll likely need to hide you two somewhere." He frowned as Tierney shook his head.

"That won't happen, Frankie. Larkin will refuse to be smothered as she calls it." Tierney locked the door after Frankie, fatigue hitting him. He walked up the stairs to his bedroom, dropping down on the bed for just a moment he thought, and fell asleep, for once sleeping until later morning. This time, he had no nightmares.

## Chapter 12

Hearing footsteps behind her as she walked in a nearby park on the Saturday, Larkin spun, not seeing anyone. This is strange, she thought. I know I'm not hearing things. She searched the area and then walked rapidly forward, heading back for the downtown area. I shouldn't be out here, not on my own, she thought. Lord, I don't know what's going on. Protect me please.

A hand grasping her arm and pulling her towards the trees had her screaming and fighting, her hands hitting at the man holding her. A lucky blow struck his face, causing his hand to loosen, and she fought her way free, running towards the street. She could hear his pounding footsteps behind her and ran faster. She didn't make it. A sudden tackle had her on the ground and then pulled to her feet and away from the street. She struggled until she felt the prick of a knife on her ribs.

Lord, please? Help me to escape. She felt her pleas were useless, but she still had to try.

Shoved into a truck, the man slid in beside her. She tried to reach to the other door but the sight of the knife in her vision stopped that. She shook with fear, not knowing who had taken her. She watched as the truck was driven away, not able to get a good look at either her attacker or the driver.

Tierney stood outside Larkin's door an hour later, not hearing her unlocking the door. He checked his watch. It was the time they were to meet. Fear suddenly hit him and he turned and rushed for the bakeshop, having seen Dave there earlier.

"Dave? I can't get an answer from Larkin."

Dave spun, and then reached for a set of keys. "I saw her earlier, heading out on a walk. She said she'd be back."

Dave tapped at the door and then unlocked it, walking up and searching. "She's not back, Tierney."

Tierney turned in a circle. "Where is she? Did she say where she was heading?"

Dave shook his head. "She just said she was going for a walk and would be back, that you were stopping by, and that you had to go somewhere. She looked thoughtful but afraid, if that makes sense."

"It does, Dave. I hadn't had a chance to warn her. Someone took a photo of us last night and left it on my desk at home."

"On your desk? How did they get in?"

"That's what Frankie wants to know. Someone had broken in yesterday when Larkin was there, but she hid. There was an officer on duty until I got home, so no one should have been able to get in."

Tierney turned and ran down the steps, searching for Larkin. "Which way was she headed?"

"Towards Gracey Park. At least, I think she was."

Dave and Tierney searched the park, with no signs of Larkin. Tierney finally pulled out his phone, calling Frankie.

"Frankie? Larkin's disappeared."

"What? When? Where? I'm downtown. Let me know where you are."

"At Gracey Park. Dave said he talked to her earlier but we had plans. It's not like her not to show up."

They searched, Frankie finally taking Tierney to his office and seating him, returning with a coffee for them both before he sank into his own chair. He watched Tierney closely.

"Tierney, what made you think she's missing?"

"Because we had plans for today. She would have called me if she couldn't make it. I know her that well." Tierney studied his hands, not willing to say what their plans were. That was not an option, he thought.

Frankie nodded before he pulled out forms to start his paperwork. "When did you see her last?"

"Last night, around nine, I think it was." Tierney looked up, worry on his face. "I didn't get a chance to tell her what we found. I was planning on that this morning."

Frankie watched him closely before he rose and closed the door. He stood against for a moment before he came and perched on the corner of his desk.

"Tierney, what is really going on?"

Tierney shrugged. "I have no idea. All I know is that I disappeared and then was rescued. Larkin was part of that." He stared at Frankie. "Do you know it was her cousins that were approached and she was specifically requested to help? Who does that?

From what she said, they just walked in and walked out with me. There were no guards."

Frankie drew a deep breath. He had known part of the story but not that. "They walked in and out? Just like that? I don't like the sounds of that."

"No. It's not pretty, I would suspect. It sounds too much like a setup to me." Tierney rose, heading for the door. "I'm sorry, Frankie. I just can't sit here and not search for her." He looked at his watch. "She's been gone for four hours. Where is she?"

"We're looking, Tierney. Abe's men are out there as well." Frankie reached for his phone as he heard a phone ringing before he realized it was Tierney's.

Tierney stared at the phone, before his eyes shot to Frankie. Frankie could hear the hope in his voice as he answered.

"Larkin? Larkin, is that you?" His eyes slid closed as she answered. "Where are you? You don't know? Are you in town?" He felt Frankie's hand on his back, shoving him towards a door and then into a car. "Talk to me, Larkin. What's around you? What's that? A quarry? Did you say a quarry?" His eyes went to Frankie, even as Frankie headed that way. "We're on our way. Are you safe?"

Frankie pulled to a stop. "This is a big area, Tierney. Can she give any idea of where she is?"

"Larkin? Larkin? I've lost her." The sorrow in his voice tugged at Frankie's heart.

Frankie turned as he heard other vehicles pulling in. "We'll start a search, Tierney. We'll find her."

Tierney stared at his phone as he heard her voice again. "She's up in a tree? What is going on? Why be up a tree?"

Frankie began to laugh, bringing Tierney's eyes to him. "Sorry, Tierney. Sounds as if she found a unique way to avoid her captors." He turned as he heard his name called.

Caleb Logan, Riverville Police Chief, stood beside Frankie, watching first Tierney, then turning to watch the activity around the quarry. "Any further word, Frankie?"

Frankie shook his head, knowing Caleb, a good friend, would be running scenarios through his mind. "She's contacted Tierney. Apparently she climbed a tree to hide."

"A tree?" Caleb stared at Frankie for a moment. "You really did say a tree? I can't say that we've ever had anyone do that before. Now, where's he going?" Caleb walked rapidly after Tierney as he headed for the quarry, Frankie beside him.

Tierney looked around, following Larkin's voice on his phone, searching for the landmarks she was giving him. He finally stood under a large maple tree, turning in a circle.

"Larkin? Is this the one?" He looked up as he heard the leaves shaking and caught sight of a sneaker. "Larkin? I'm right below you." His phone in his pocket, he reached to touch her foot, causing her to jerk it back.

"Tierney? Is that really you?"

"It is, my love. Keep moving down. I'll catch you. I promise you I will."

---

"Oh, you can't. You're not strong enough yet." Her voice was growing louder as she moved towards him. "Watch out of the way and I'll drop. I've done it plenty of times before."

He caught her as she jumped from the tree. "My love, I was so scared." His arms tightened around her even as he heard Caleb and Frankie walking towards them. "Are you okay?"

"I am, now." She leaned back to look up at him. "I have no idea who they were or what they wanted." She peeked around him at the other two men. "And you went to Frankie, didn't you?"

"What was I to do? You were missing and I had to find you." He turned to face the two officers, an arm tight around her.

Caleb watched the two closely before he spoke. "Larkin, we'll need to get your statement. But I must say, you were wise to climb a tree. No one would think of looking up."

She smirked for a moment. "I had practice. That's how I used to hide on Lincoln and Logan. They never figured it out."

## Chapter 13

Larkin glared at Frankie as he questioned her, refusing to answer his questions. Tierney watched, knowing she was at her limit.

"Frankie, can she just say what happened, sign her statement, and then leave? She's at her limit or past it." Tierney was perched on the arm of Larkin's chair, his hand on her shoulder.

Frankie looked up. "I think we've got all we need. I'm sorry, Larkin. You0 just need to understand that sometimes we go back over statements and sentences and words, just to make sure we have everything." Reaching for the printer, he handed her the sheaf of papers. "Just read it over, initial all the pages but the last and then sign and date the last page. That should work."

Larkin sighed. "I'm sorry, Frankie. This has not been one of my better days. It was not how I planned to spend it."

She rose, heading away from Frankie, leaving Tierney to have a few words with him before he ran after her, catching her hand with his and leading her towards her apartment.

She stopped suddenly, her hand pulling Tierney to a halt. "We were to meet with Greg today. It's past that time now. Oh, what will we do?"

He shrugged. "I called him when you were talking with Frankie. He asked if we would come for supper. He'll talk with us then, he said." He watched her face closely. "He's fine with that, as long as we are."

She finally nodded, walking forward again. "I need to change. I have to throw out these clothes. I can't keep them." She sighed. "Who did this, Tierney?"

"I have no idea. There's something we need to talk about." He followed her up the stairs to her apartment, heading for the kitchen. "Go and change. I'll start some coffee, your tea, and find us something to eat."

She stood for a moment before she hugged him and then walked away, a thoughtful look on her face. Lord, what I am to do? Those men threatened him and I can't let them hurt him. Oh, Lord, please. Keep him safe. My heart couldn't take it if he is hurt again.

She turned for a moment, not quite sure what to wear. She finally pulled on jeans and a light sweater, hoping it was suitable. She sighed. She never used to worry about how she looked. She studied her face, seeing the dark shadows under her eyes, the scratches from her run through the trees, and knew that Tierney needed to know what happened, but that he wouldn't ask. He would wait for her to tell him. This is so different, Lord. With Dad, Lincoln and Logan, they would have demanded I tell them what happened. They would not have let me clean up first. Well, maybe, they might have but they would not have been happy. I can see Lincoln and Logan changing somewhat, but Lord, please, let them understand I can't have them running my life anymore, even if they say they care and they do it out of love for me.

Tierney turned as he heard her feet moving across the tile floor and simply enveloped her into a hug, his very touch calming her. She finally stepped back, heading for the kitchen before his hand stopped her.

"Living room, Larkin. You need to sit and put your feet up." He shook his head as she still tried to head for the kitchen. "I've put our meal in there. I hope that was okay. You need to be comforted and be comfortable."

She paused. "You're right. There's nothing wrong with eating in there, is there?" She turned and headed for her favourite corner of the couch, watching as he dropped down beside her, reaching for her hand.

He prayed for her and then for them both, before he handed her the plate he had fixed for her. She looked at it and sighed.

"I'm not really hungry, Tierney. What time do we have to be at Greg's?"

"It's only one, Larkin. He said around six works." He studied her. "Can you tell me more of what happened? I had the feeling you didn't tell Frankie everything."

She nodded, shoving the plate back at him and reaching for her cup of tea. "I didn't. I just couldn't."

She huddled down in her corner, knowing she had to tell him, but afraid to do just that. Her friendship with him was still so fresh and young and uncertain, no matter what decision they had made.

She began to speak, asking that he not interrupt her, or she wouldn't be able to finish.

She had spoken with Dave early that morning, taking his teasing in the vein he meant it, promising to stop in for some pastries when she returned from her walk. She headed along the street, towards the park she loved to walk through, not seeing the truck that followed her. She strode through the paths, a freedom washing over her that she had not felt in years, a lightening of her whole being, she thought. What Tierney had offered her was freedom but also safety. Friendship and she prayed love at some point. She had spent the night in prayer, knowing she needed to seek God's will for the step they were contemplating.

She turned back towards the entrance, not seeing the men who approached her, not until she was grabbed. She fought to escape, finally gaining her freedom, her feet carrying her away from the man. That was, until he tackled her and pulled her to her feet. She felt the knife against her and still struggled, even as she was shoved into the truck. She reached for the other door, intending on escaping until she felt the knife tip once more at her side, this time digging in a bit. She stopped her struggling and watched instead, praying she would have a chance to escape. She frowned as they only went a short way out of the town, towards where she knew the quarry was.

As she heard Tierney's name, she listened closer, hearing the plans they had to use her to trap him. She knew she had to get away, but how she wasn't sure. As the truck stopped, an argument broke out between the man beside her and the front seat passenger, growing heated as they fought over just where to put her until they could reach Tierney. She edged closer to the door, finding the knife had fallen away from her.

A sudden movement on her part had the door shoved open and she landed outside on her feet, running towards the quarry and safety, she prayed. She heard the yells and anger and curses from behind her and picked up her pace. She searched, her head twisting and turned as she looked for just the right spot, her breath coming in gasps as she ran before she spied what she wanted. All those years as a girl of climbing trees just had to pay off, she thought. She jumped for the lower branch and then pulled herself up on it, scrambling to climb higher, finally sitting on a branch, her arms wrapped around the trunk, praying they had not seen her.

She heard them searching for her before they left. She listened and thought she heard the truck drive way. How long had it been, she wondered, not having her watch on. She twisted around, pulling out her phone, gazing at the clock. That long? She didn't think it had been that long, but she guessed it had been. She searched her contact list, finding Tierney's number, hesitating before she dialed, hearing his beloved voice coming through to her. She fought back sobs as she talked to him, trying to be as clear as she could.

She finally heard him calling her, moving down the tree, jumping back up a branch as he touched her foot. She spoke to him, not sure afterwards what she had said, before she dropped from the branch, into his arms and was held tight. She could feel the fear he had had for her.

—

## Chapter 14

Tierney had listened to her statement and knew from what she had just told him that she had not said everything to Frankie. He sighed. She needed to but he knew she would refuse.

"Do you remember anything about them, other than what you told Frankie?"

She shook her head. "Not really. I wasn't paying that much attention to them. I was more concerned in finding a way to escape." She turned to him. "They were after you. They said that. But they didn't say why."

"I know that, Larkin, but someone is also after you." He sighed again. "When I got home last night, there was an envelope on my desk. A picture of us, out for dinner. They were watching us last night."

Her face whitened. "Last night? How did it get into your home?"

"That's what we don't know. There was an officer there until I got home. Frankie was going to talk to him, but I don't know if he has yet. He didn't say." Tierney's head went back as he looked up. "Where do we go, Larkin, where you'll be safe?"

She shrugged. "It's not me I'm worried about. It's you. I can't figure out why they want you." Her head went back as an image flitted through her mind. "Tierney, do you have a manuscript that you were given about three months ago, one they wanted you to verify as authentic?"

He nodded. "I have several that I was asked to look at. Why do you ask?"

"Because somehow that keeps coming to my mind. That you have a manuscript that isn't old or right or something and they want you to say it is." She looked over at him. "Can they do that?"

"They can try, but I don't know if I have one." He rose and began to pace. "I have a number I have been working on. The ones I received about three or four months ago? They're in the line to be researched. But I have a number ahead of them." His voice died away. "You're thinking they will try and force me to authenticate one?"

She nodded. "I think so." She looked over at the clock. "Do you realize how late it is? We've been talking all afternoon. And I never did get downstairs to get the pastries Dave told me to." She sounded disgruntled at that.

"He'll have more, I'm sure." He reached for the tray, heading to the kitchen, tidying everything away as she watched.

"You didn't have to."

"But I did. That's how I was raised. I make a mess, I clean it up."

She tilted her head to study him. "You've never talked about your childhood or your family."

He shrugged. "I never had one. My parents both died from overdoses when I was just weeks old. I ended up in foster care and that stigma meant I didn't get adopted. My foster family was great but they just couldn't adopt me. I still don't understand why but I've come to accept that." He turned and reached for her hand. "Do you need a jacket or anything?"

She shook her head. "No, I'm good. Are we really sure we want to meet with Greg?"

"We are. We talk to him and then we walk away and discuss it between us. No one knows anything until we decide to tell them."

Greg and Mary Evans exchanged glances with one another before they watched the younger couple. Their son and daughter were away with their grandparents and they were glad, just for once, that they were. Greg finally pointed to the living room.

"Why don't we sit in there? Mary?"

"That's fine. I'll bring in the coffee and dessert." She frowned at Larkin. "Do you drink coffee?"

Larkin shook her head. "No, I'm sorry. Do you have tea?"

"That we do."

Greg listened as Tierney explained what had transpired with him, how Larkin had gotten involved and what she had faced that very day before he shook his head.

"We were praying that the adventures our friends have had were over. It certainly doesn't sound like that." He eyed them. "But that's not why you wanted to talk to me."

Tierney shared a look with Larkin before he shook his head. "It's not. This is what we have decided." He explained their discussion and what their decision had been, knowing from friends that

Greg would listen to them and then advise them according to what God led him to do.

Greg shared a look with Mary before he nodded at Tierney, asking questions as to why and how. He finally sat back, his eyes on his hands before he looked at them.

"This is not something I know you're walking into lightly. Having said that, I do need to pray over this. It's not a decision I can give you tonight. I have done this before, with two couples, but there was a love developing already between them. Perhaps you need to speak with them." He reached for a paper, writing down some names. "The first one, believe it or not, is the police chief in Elmton. He has quite a story. The second one is the pastor of the church there. He and his wife also have a story to tell. Talk to them. If you want, I can set something up for you."

Tierney pocketed the paper, his eyes on Larkin, who was watching Mary. "Larkin?" When she turned to him, he spoke. "Are you okay with this?"

She nodded, not letting him know she was relieved. "I am. I think we need to wait. I mean, we've made the decision that we want to marry, but we can't just rush into. Can we?"

Mary began to laugh, bringing Larkin's eyes to her. "You sounded so definite there, Larkin. Why don't we meet again Tuesday night and discuss this? Greg?"

"That works, Mary, unless the Good Lord lets me know by service time tomorrow we can go ahead. Let me pray with you two now, though."

---

Larkin paced her living room after Tierney left, only a low light on, the drapes closed tightly. She was afraid in a way she had never been afraid in her life. She knew something was going to happen but she just didn't know what. She jumped as her phone chimed and she reached for it, a sigh coming from her as she saw Lincoln's number. She set her phone back down, letting his call go to voice mail. She needed to talk to her family but she wasn't sure what to say.

When the phone rang again, she stared at it, peering at the name. Lincoln, again, she thought, finally reaching to answer.

"Larkin?" Lincoln sounded relieved to hear her voice. "I've been worried about you all day. That something had happened to you. Are you okay?"

"I am, now."

Lincoln hesitated before he asked. "Now? Did something happen today?"

She blew out a breath, knowing she could talk to him, at least, without him wanting too badly to pack her up and move her home. "There did. Lincoln, you have to promise me. You have to promise you won't tell Dad. He'll want me to move back home and I can't do that."

"I promise, Larkin, but you're worrying me. What happened?"

She dropped to the floor, her back against the couch, her legs stretched out in front of her as she crossed her ankles. "Please, Lincoln. Just let me tell you. But I know you're going to want to ride in and take over. I can't let you do that. I am an adult and I need to be able to make my own decisions."

"And we haven't let you, have we? Holly picked up on that, love, and told me we needed to let you breathe, is how she put it. Has it been that bad?"

"It has. I know you love me and want me to be safe, but I need to be my own person. That's part of why I moved away from home."

"I'm sorry, Larkin. I never knew it was that bad. I wish I had. I think Dad is just so worried about you, he doesn't realize how he's acting." He paused, thoughts running through his mind. "Let me talk to Dad. Maybe he'll understand better. Logan says you haven't talked to him."

"No." She sounded grumpy. "He's almost as bad as Dad."

Lincoln laughed. "He is at that. But he is trying to change. Aveleen's working on him." There was silence for a moment. "Now, tell me what happened today. And I already know I'm not going to like what I hear. Was Tierney there for you?"

"He was, eventually. I went for a walk in my favourite park, was abducted, got away, climbed a tree and then Tierney and the police were there. They've threatened him, Lincoln. I don't know why, but they've threatened him. And yesterday when I was working, someone broke into his home and tried to find me. I hid."

There was silence for a few moments as Lincoln tried to control his emotions, Holly's arm around him as she heard what Larkin had said.

"Are you okay, Larkin?" Lincoln's voice was barely above a whisper.

---

"I am, Lincoln. Tierney found me and brought me home." She blinked back tears as she rubbed at her leg and then a finger flicked at the material of her jeans. "I don't know what I would do without him."

Lincoln spoke in a hesitant manner. "Larkin, I'm going to ask something, and you don't have to answer. Just think about it, okay? You're my little sister. I love you dearly. My greatest wish, after you loving God as much as you can, is that you find someone to love and who loves you more than himself. If Tierney is that man, and he decides he wants to spend the rest of his life with you, accept him. If he's not, then God will provide you with an answer and with the man you are to spend your life with. That's how we're praying for you." He stopped, overcome by the emotions of what his sister went through. "You are okay?"

"I guess." She shrugged without thinking, forgetting that he couldn't see her. "I talked to an officer here and the police chief too. Then Tierney and I talked it through." She didn't mention the meeting with Greg. That was too much of an uncertainty as to their plans. "Lincoln, how did you know you were being chased?"

"I can't tell you that, Larkin. I didn't know I was. I just had a feeling that someone was after me." He paused, thinking back over what he and Holly had gone through. "All I can say is this. Stay close to Tierney. Keep in contact with the police. Make sure you're aware of what's going on around you. Your apartment? Is it safe?"

She began to laugh. "It is. Dave, the owner, and his wife, Rylee, have made sure of that. They

---

even put in a camera doorbell for me so I can see who's at the door."

"That's good. You said Dave and Rylee?"

"I did. How's Holly and your little one?"

"They're great. The little one is growing so fast. You need to see her."

"I'm not coming there. You need to come here." She stopped. "No, that won't work. If you do, then Dad and Mom will have to come, and Logan will have to find me."

"He already has, Larkin. He knows where you're living. He saw you one day but he didn't want to approach you. He's very uncertain about you right now."

"I'm sorry, Lincoln. There's just been something going on now for months. That's another reason I wanted to move, but it seems as if trouble followed me." She looked at the clock. "I have to run, Lincoln. It's getting late and Tierney said he'd be here early."

## *Chapter 15*

Tierney searched through the manuscripts he had waiting for him to research, a frown on his face, before he turned to Larkin.

"Larkin? Do you have any idea what the manuscript was about?"

She spun as he spoke, her chair giving a soft squeak and crinkle of leather. "I think it was…Now, what was it?" She approached him. "Can I look or is that not allowed?"

"You can look. I'm trying to think which one it would have been." He turned back to the metal boxes they were stored in, looking at the labels with the dates. "How long ago do you think it was?"

"I think likely well before you were taken captive. How long have you had these?"

"These ones here?" He pointed to a stack. "These three for about a year. People understand that it takes time and research." He reached for one, a frown on his face. "I don't remember anything odd, though."

She opened one of the boxes he had pointed to and stopped. "Tierney. This one. This sounds like the name."

He stood beside her, reading. "The Mythical Magic. That is an odd name." He reached for cotton gloves and then gently lifted out the manuscript. "There is something odd about it. It just doesn't look old."

---

93

She nodded. "Can we look through it?"

He nodded, handing her a pair of gloves. "Wear these." He reached for a camera. "I need you to videotape this one. I don't usually, but this time I think I do."

She watched as he worked through the manuscript, carefully turning each page before he stopped at the centre, staring at the envelope laying there. "I didn't open this, just put it away. I was too involved in another one at the time. I wonder what this is."

He lifted out the envelope and laid it on the table they were working at, somehow knowing this would change their lives in a drastic way. He searched Larkin's face, waiting until she nodded before he reached for it once more, pulling out the tucked-in flap and then dumping out the paper inside. He frowned as he unfolded it.

"This is definitely not old. It's only printed on one side. This is computer done, Larkin, I can tell that. Someone tried to make it look old but it's not. The envelope is a giveaway on that. Can you get a close up of this?" He waited as she did, before he stood once more staring down at this. "This is not good, Larkin. This is not good at all."

"What do you mean?" She had a puzzled look on her face as she stared at him.

"What I mean is this. This is modern, which makes me suspect the manuscript is as well." He turned back to the manuscript, leafing through it. "It's modern. The paper has the wrong feel to it. I can see where someone tried to age it and it didn't

—

work.  The font is wrong too.  It's not handwritten.  I can tell that."  He stood back, hand rubbing at his cheek, eyes thoughtful.  "So, why give such an obvious fake to me?"

"I don't like this, Tierney.  Something is wrong."  She set the camera down and pulled out her phone.  "We need to talk to Frankie or someone there."

He sighed.  "That we do.  Put your phone away, Larkin.  I'll make the call."

Larkin stood back from the door for Frankie to enter, followed by a crime scene tech.  She raised an eyebrow at him in question.

He grinned.  "Preemptive thinking.  Trouble is following you two around, just like everyone else."

Frankie watched as Tierney explained his findings before nodding at the tech, who moved forward.

"Do we need to watch for anything, Tierney?"

"I suspect not.  It's too modern for me to even consider looking at.  There is one thing, though."  He turned to stare at the manuscript.  "There is something off about it.  And I'm not sure what."

"How be we take it?  Then we can put out a news release that you have turned over a fake manuscript to the police and that we're investigating.  That might make them back off."  Frankie turned to the letter.  "Now, this letter?"

"This letter.  It's a bunch of gibberish.  It doesn't make sense.  It's like they tried to make it sound old, but weren't sure how they talked two

---

hundred years ago. And if I remember correctly, that's what they told me." He moved to stand beside Larkin, a frown on his face. "Larkin?"

She suddenly spun, her eyes huge, her hands going to her mouth. "It was you! You were there. And so was a couple. A young man and an older woman. It was in Hope."

Tierney nodded. "That's correct. About a year or more ago. I told them I had too many in front of them to take it but they insisted I take it. Now, I have to wonder why."

Frankie had been watching them and then reached for the letter. "I see what you mean, Tierney. It doesn't make sense, unless it's in code of some kind." He dropped it into an evidence bag, signed and dated the bag, and then handed it off to a tech. "Anything else we need to know?"

Tierney and Larkin shared a look and then shook their heads.

"No, not really." Tierney spoke even as he caught Larkin's look and frowned. Now, what was up with her, he wondered.

"Okay, then. Stay safe, you two. I'll let you know what we find out about this." He paused. "Larkin, you are okay after the other day?"

She shrugged. "I have no idea, Frankie. And until you find whoever it was, I'll be looking over my shoulder." She walked away, leaving the men to stare after her.

"She's hurting, Frankie, and not just on her part. She's been drawn into my life, against her will, by someone we can't identify. That makes it really hard on her."

"I hear you. Logan says she hasn't been in touch."

"And she won't, not until she's ready." Tierney sighed. "There's a history there, Frankie, that's not mine to share. But she did talk to Lincoln Saturday night."

"Well, that's good." Frankie walked away, leaving Tierney to stare around him and then head out to find Larkin.

"Larkin?"

She spun, a shuttered look on her face. "We can go back to work now?"

"We can." He squinted at his watch. "But first, lunch. It's that time of day."

## Chapter 16

Watching Larkin closely, Tierney finally stepped in her way to stop her pacing. She frowned at him and moved around him. He sighed. There was no easy way to do this, he thought.

"Larkin?"

She turned as he spoke and moved back towards him. "Who did this, Tierney? Who is setting you up?"

"Would you recognize the couple of you saw them again?"

She shrugged. "I might, but I don't think I got that close a look at them. Is that what this is all about?"

"I have no idea." He glanced at the clock. "We were to meet with Greg tonight."

She shook her head. "I don't think I can. Not yet, Tierney. I'm sorry." She turned and ran from the room and he heard the front door close softly behind her.

He ran after her, catching up as she hit the sidewalk by the street, his hand stopping her.

"Don't run from me, Larkin. I understand. We can wait." He looked around. "Let me drive you home, at least."

She broke away from and ran, tears on her cheeks. He stood for a moment, hand in the air to stop her, and then ran after her, once more stopping her, his hand on her arm.

"Larkin, please, don't run from me, ever. I can't handle it if you disappear again."

She turned to look at him, a shuttered look coming over her face again, even as she wiped at the tears on her cheeks. "I'm sorry, Tierney. I know we talked about this, but I can't. Not with whatever it is hanging over our heads."

"Again, I understand. I still think we should talk to Greg. He can advise us."

"You're not giving up, are you?" Frustrated, she looked behind him and then screamed. "Tierney, look out." Her hand grasped his arm and pulled him towards the lawn of the house next to his, tumbling down and taking him with her. She felt the heat of the vehicle motor as it missed them.

Tierney sat up abruptly, his arms around her, even as he looked for the vehicle. "It's gone!"

"It is. Oh, Tierney, it was aiming right for you. You could have been killed."

"I don't get it. Frankie was putting out that notice for us. I think this has gone beyond that."

"Unless there are two parties. And I somehow think there are." She stood, her hand out for him to grasp, holding tight as he steadied himself on his feet. "You're hurt."

"No, just shaken. That's all. You're okay?"

She nodded and then looked around. "I guess we should go talk to Greg, after all. I can't handle this, not knowing when I'll see you for the last time."

---

He grinned at her phrasing. "And we shall. Come on back to the house. We need to tidy up a bit."

Greg watched the young couple before he glanced up at Mary, who was watching them intently.

"Larkin. Tierney. I understand what you two are going through, to some extent. I just want to clarify that you are taking this step on your own free will, both of you, and not being pushed by anyone."

"We are, Greg." Tierney's hand tightened on Larkin's. "We are."

Greg nodded. "Then, I have prayed about it. I'm not happy that you two aren't in love, but I have not been told to refuse to marry you." He shook his head. "And God would have stopped this. When were you two thinking of the ceremony?"

"Within the next week, I guess." Larkin looked at Tierney. "Excuse me. Mary, can I talk to you? On our own?" She fought back tears, not quite sure why.

The men stood and watched the ladies leave, and then seated themselves again. Greg watched Tierney closely and then nodded. He's in love, isn't he, Lord? And he just doesn't know how to tell her without her thinking he's just saying that to get her to marry him.

"Greg? What do I do?" Tierney rose and walked to the window, staring out before he spun around. "How do I keep her safe?"

"At this point, Tierney, I'm not sure you have any good options. They've shown they are bold enough to walk into your own home." Greg paused, his eyes narrowing as he thought. "No, that won't work."

"What won't work? Please, if you have any ideas, tell me." Tierney sat back down across from Greg, almost pleading with him.

"I was going to suggest you two change names and move away, but they would still find you."

Tierney stared at him for a moment before he caught the glint of mischief on Greg's face and grinned. "We could try that. Larkin's already moved towns. Where would you suggest?"

Greg began to laugh. "Somehow, I don't think that would work. And putting her away safely would not likely work."

"That definitely would not. She has felt smothered for years by her father and her brothers. She said she finally talked to Lincoln and he was going to talk to their father and Logan."

Greg nodded. "So, then, what are your plans? You do have some, don't you?"

Tierney shook his head. "Frankly, I am not sure. I don't do this, you know. I work with manuscripts, not this kind of stuff."

Greg began to laugh harder. "Then, I guess we need to talk to some people for you."

Mary watched as Larkin paced the yard, her hand trailing across the flowers, before she spoke.

"Larkin?" When the younger woman turned, Mary continued. "Are you sure? This is a big step."

"I know it is. I'm sure. When he was almost run down today, I realized how important he is to me." She looked up at the sky, trying to compose herself.

"God knows, I need him in my life and not just to make sure he's safe and I'm safe."

"That's what we've picked up from you both, Greg and I. There is an attraction there, isn't there?" When Larkin nodded, Mary hugged her. "Then, we need to make some plans. You'll want your family involved."

Larkin looked at her in horror. "Absolutely not. Tierney and I talked about it. Mom would take over, Dad would play the heavy, and Logan would be right there at Dad's side."

"But what about Lincoln? What would he do?"

"He gave me his blessing Saturday night, if you can believe it."

Mary nodded. "Then, let's go back in and see what we need to do. A dress, I think, and flowers and a meal?"

Larkin stared at her. "I really don't know. I'm not sure." She blew out a breath that fluttered her bangs. "This is so definite, isn't it?"

Mary laughed again, as arm around Larkin, they walked to the house. "This is your day, my dear. What you want is what you get. If you need a dress, I think mine would fit you just about right. My daughter would be glad to share."

"She would? She doesn't know me."

Tierney watched Larkin later that night as he drove her home. "Are you really okay with this, my love?"

She nodded. "My family won't understand, and I don't know how to explain it to them. It will hurt them that they're not here but if they are, they'll take over and smother me."

## Chapter 17

Lincoln stood at the back of the church, Holly beside him, as he watched Larkin walk towards him, a questioning look on her face, before he reached to hug his sister, holding on for just a bit.

"Lincoln? What are you doing here?"

"Tierney called me, just to talk. He let slip, without meaning to, that today was your day. I had to come. Please forgive me."

She stepped back, her eyes on him and then on Holly, who nodded. "I'm glad you're here. I just wish it had been different, that Mom and Dad and Logan could be here."

Holly hugged Larkin, her eyes on her face, before she spoke. "May I make a suggestion, and it's only a suggestion? Call them and do a live video of some kind. That way, they're part of it but you still have it the way you want."

Larkin stared at her and then at Lincoln. "Could we? I don't want to exclude them, but I just can't have them here. It's too dangerous for one thing." She groaned. "Logan won't forgive me."

Lincoln hugged her. "We still have, what an hour or so? Let me find him and bring Aveleen and him here. Please?"

She finally nodded. "Okay. But who sets up the video?"

"I will."

She spun at the voice behind her and saw one of Abe's men standing there. "What is going on? Tierney!"

Tierney wrapped her in his arms from behind. "It's okay, my love. We're not taking over, we're not making you do anything you don't want. These are suggestions that are being made. It is up to you. If you want, we'll run away and get married somewhere else."

She finally shook her head, sighing. "I guess we can. I just know Mom and Dad will never forgive me. Mom has planned for this day all my life, and has refused to listen to me."

A hour later, video feed set up, Lincoln called his parents, asking that they turn to a certain program on their computer. He refused to say why, saying it was not his to tell. He reached for his sister, hugging her, knowing she was near tears at the way the day was turning out.

"Larkin, let me walk you to him."

She stared up a him, shock on her face. "I never even thought about that, you know."

None of them saw the forms that stood at the rear of the church, watching before they slipped out. Larkin studied the people who had gathered, knowing they had chosen to be there. She knew Abe's men and their ladies but there were others she didn't know, but that Abe had said were friends of theirs. She spied Frankie and his wife to one side and he nodded at her. Relief flowed through her that they cared enough to come but that he was there, bringing a sense of safety to her.

105

Neither Tierney or Larkin could describe the ceremony after, other than it was not what they had planned or expected. Larkin hadn't spoken to her parents, but Logan had. As he hugged her, he apologized for how he had treated her, vowing to do better. Aveleen had been working on him as well. He said he had talked to their parents, and they had been disappointed not to be part of her day, but they were glad she had found someone.

Tierney turned at last, reaching for her hand, walking her out of the church through a back door and tucking her into his car. They were headed to her apartment first, he said. He felt the tingling in his neck and looked around, knowing someone was there but not sure where or who. He didn't see Frankie watching him before he too walked around the church, joined by Abe's men, searching for those after Tierney or Larkin or both of them. No one was quite sure who they were after anymore.

Turning as Tierney approached her later that night, a cup of tea in his hand for her, she thanked him, not quite sure how to respond. He simply hugged her and walked her outside to the yard, twilight deepening around them.

"Tomorrow, I need to head for the library in Oak City to do some research. I go every few weeks. Or at least I did." He was exhausted, and having trouble thinking. "I would like it if you came."

"I want to. I don't want to stay here on my own, not if I can help it. I'm afraid, Tierney. Afraid he'll be back."

"I know. I'm afraid for you as well." His arm around her shoulders tightened. "I like to leave early in the morning. I found a really nice place to breakfast in. I would like to share that with you."

She nodded, her eyes on her hands. "Why this ring, Tierney?"

"Which one?"

"Either one, I guess." She touched the ruby and emerald engagement ring. "This is an unusual combination."

"It is. There's a history there. I think I told you it was my foster mother's. She gave it to me years ago, for my special lady she said. She shared so much with me. I need to take you to meet them sometime. Anyway, the ruby she said is to remind me that God thinks a wife is a very good thing for a man to have, that her price is far above rubies. And the emerald is to remind us we need to keep growing together as a couple, that if we don't, we stagnate and our love would die." He paused, groaning. "That's what she told me. I'm sorry, Larkin. I didn't mean to hurt you."

She nodded, too unsure of how he felt to say anything.

The next morning, Tierney looked up from his research, watching as Larkin read through what he had written.

"This is interesting, Tierney. How do you know this?"

He reached for her hand, tilting it so he could see what she had been reading. "I have no idea. I just know what to look for." He looked around, feeling uncomfortable and knowing they needed to get on the road soon. "It just comes to me. Listen. About that manuscript that Frankie took?"

"Oh, that one. What about it?"

"I still think it so strange. Has Frankie said anything?"

"No, he hasn't. But come to think of it, he does want to meet with us this afternoon." He sighed as he studied his notes and then began to tidy them together, stuffing them into his briefcase. "We'll need to head out, I guess. I'll have to come back next week again."

She nodded. "We can do that. I need to be getting at the mail, anyway. You haven't let me see it for a couple of days."

He grinned. "I haven't? Well, then, off we go."

## Chapter 18

Frankie watched as Tierney dug through his desk, looking for the document he knew he had related to the manuscript. Larkin watched him for a while before she shook her head, walked to the filing cabinet and pulled out a file, dropping it on the desk in front of him.

Tierney paused, his eyes on the folder, before his hands reached to open it.

"You are ahead of me, my love. When did you file this?"

"One of the first days I worked for you. All your paperwork is filed, under the name of the manuscript, with a secondary file under the client name. They are also in a database on your computer." She laughed at the look on his face. "It's what I do, Tierney. I organize. That's part of it." She stabbed a finger at the folder. "Now, Frankie's waiting."

Frankie couldn't hide his grin, knowing that Larkin had politely put Tierney in his place without him realizing it.

"Okay, Tierney. What can you tell me?"

Larkin handed him a folder. "I took the liberty of having Tierney sign a waiver and copied the folder." When Tierney just stared at her, she shook her head. "We talked about it, Tierney. You told me to go ahead."

"I did? I guess I did after all." He spun in his chair, his eyes on Frankie. "What can you tell us?"

"Not a whole lot more than what you told me. The techs think it's a code of some kind but they can't decipher it, not yet."

"We have a copy, don't we still, Larkin? Then we can work on it as well. Some of the old books do have a code in them. They can be hard to find, even when you're looking for it and you've done it before." He took the folder she handed him. "This is great, Larkin. Thank you."

Frankie shook his head again, knowing Tierney was lost to them. He beckoned to Larkin and she followed him from the room.

"You'll not get him out of that manuscript now."

She laughed. "That's okay. Maybe he'll figure it out in the first few pages and this will be all over."

"I wish that were true." Frankie looked around and then reached to hug her. "I know why you two did what you did, but forgive me for meddling. I've watched Tierney. He loves you, don't ever doubt that. He's not the type of man to offer you marriage if he didn't think it would be for your lifetime and especially if he hadn't prayed it through."

"Thank you, Frankie. Your words help." She bit at her lip. "This is so new to me, you know, having all these people I can be friends with. I've feeling overwhelmed."

"Don't let the ladies do that to you. Get to know them and then find the ones you can be better friends with. That's what we've all done. Deirdre's friends with them all but she is closer to some of them than others. Speaking of which, she has asked if she can call you and arrange a dinner with the four of us."

Larkin studied him and then nodded. "I would like that, provided it doesn't put you in danger."

Frankie stared at her and then began to laugh. "You haven't heard? We had an adventure as we all call it before we married. My wife is very scary, I'll have you know. She worked on missions overseas and the men and boys taught her how to defend herself well. We'll tell you our story when we have dinner. Just watch your vehicle. She likes to take the valve caps."

Larkin began to laugh. "I think I need to hear that story."

Tierney finally looked up as he felt Larkin's hand on his shoulder. "Did you want something?"

"Yes. I have our dinner ready. You need to set this aside, Tierney. Enough for the day."

He looked at her, looked at the paperwork, and then back up at her before he tidied the piles and rose, reaching to turn off the desk lamp he didn't remember turning on. "You're right. I can't work all the time, not anymore."

"No, you can't. You're still recovering from what you went through." She walked back towards the kitchen, reaching for the casserole she had prepared and heading for the dining room. "I hope you don't mind eating in here. Just for tonight?" She was hesitant and he just swept her into a hug.

"I will eat wherever you set my food. That's a given."

Three days later, Larkin paused in her work, her eyes on the letter she had just opened, before they raised to Tierney. She reached for her phone, quietly called Frankie, to let him know they had a threatening letter and just what did he want her to do with it, besides burn it?

Tierney had looked up as he heard her voice rising and then rose, coming to sit on the corner of her desk and reaching for the letter, a chill running through him at the threat contained in it. He shifted to look at his desk. He thought he had found a clue in the manuscript but he wasn't quite sure.

Larkin shoved herself back from the desk and moved rapidly towards his desk, anger sparking from her.

"Enough is enough, Tierney. First they almost kill you. And now they threaten to do just that." She stabbed a finger at the pile of paper. "Have you found anything yet?"

He rose as he heard the doorbell. "I'll be right back. I think I have."

He returned, Frankie and Caleb following him. Caleb studied Larkin, not quite sure what to think of her. He hadn't gotten to know her yet, and wondered at the swiftness of their marriage.

"Frankie, take that piece of paper, please. I want it out of here." Larkin stood, arms wrapped around herself, still angry at the threat.

Caleb bit back a grin, shaking his head. "Tierney, Frankie said you were working through the manuscript as well?"

"I am. I think I may have found the clue." He turned, catching himself as his head spun. Frankie's hand on his arm kept him from falling before he shoved him down into his chair.

Larkin's eyes narrowed. She knew he hadn't been sleeping, she had heard him moving around in his bedroom during the nights. She sighed. He wouldn't let her know, now would he?

"Tierney, what clue did you find?" Frankie's voice cut through the haze he felt.

"This. There is a common theme running through the manuscript. The wording is different in places and I think that's the clue. I have to study it more." He spun to his computer. "If I drop the sentences into a program, it may decipher or decode them."

Larkin's hand on his stopped him. "We can work on that tomorrow, Tierney. What have you discovered so far? I think that is what Frankie and Caleb are asking."

"You're right. So far, it looks as if it's instructions for something. Just what I'm not sure. Not drugs or anything like that. It's almost as if it's directions to some treasure, but I have no idea what."

Caleb nodded as he watched Larkin, seeing her frown at something Tierney said. "Larkin? What did you remember?"

She spun to watch him. "How did you know I had?"

He simply grinned at her as Frankie began to laugh. "It's okay, Larkin. He does that all the time. But tell us. You've remembered something."

She nodded, her eyes on Tierney who was absorbed in the manuscript. "I did. I remember seeing Tierney with the couple. A younger man. An older lady. They had the manuscript with them that day. It was in Hope." She began to tap her chin with her finger. "But where in Hope?"

Tierney looked up. "I met them at a cafe, I think, and then we headed to a used book store. Then back to the cafe." He leaned back in his chair. "I had forgotten that. How did I do that?"

"It was likely buried with what you went through." Caleb sank into a chair, his eyes shifting between the two. "What else have you remembered and not told us?"

Larkin spun to stare at him, catching the smile he sent her way, before she relaxed. "I'm not used to someone like you, Chief Logan. I am really."

"For starters, we'll be friends. It's a given. So it's Caleb. Hannah is cousin to Logan's wife, so in a way we're family. We just haven't gotten to know you and we want to rectify that. Hannah's going to be calling you to set up a time for meal. No pressure." His hand went up to stop her words. "We're not intruding on the newlyweds. We just want you to know we care about you, pray for you, and want to get to know both of you better." He sighed. "And somehow I think that is going to happen, whether we want it to or not."

Franke began to laugh. "Isn't that how it went with all our friends?"

Caleb frowned at him. "It did and it was supposed to stop."

Larkin and Tierney began to laugh as well.

"We'll try to stop it, Caleb, but I'm not sure how successful we'll be." Tierney turned back to his paperwork. "Frankie, have your techs come up with anything?"

"Not really, but then they haven't had a lot of time work on it."

"That's okay. I think I have what they'll need." He quickly printed off his notes and handed them to Frankie. "Here. This should be what they need. The race is on to see who solves it first."

Frankie shook his head. "Somehow, I expect you two will win."

Caleb stood, his eyes moving between the two. "I don't need to warn you two to stay safe. Be aware of what's around you all the time. Call if you need us."

## Chapter 19

Larkin was uneasy as she walked through the downtown area towards her apartment. She needed to pack it up, but was hesitant to and she had no idea why. Tierney hadn't asked if she had but he was aware of her hesitation. He had watched as Larkin had walked away that day, not saying anything, just alert to any danger around her.

Larkin spun in a circle in her apartment, frowning. She had no idea where to start. She had taken her clothes and any personal items already. That just left her furniture. She wasn't attached to it. She ran for the stairs, heading for the bakeshop, hoping Dave or Rylee would be there.

Dave looked up as he heard the door, drying his hands on a towel before he walked towards Larkin.

"Larkin? You look like a lady on a mission. What can I do for you?"

"Dave, I've moved everything I want from the apartment. I mean, my personal stuff. There's the furniture, though. I don't know what to do with it."

"Leave it for now. I can always rent it furnished. That way, if you do decide you want anything from it, it's there." He held up a hand at her protest. "It works for both of us, benefits us both. Now, come through to the kitchen. Rylee thought you might be through today. She left some goodies for you."

"She did? She shouldn't have. Can I come back for them? I have a couple of errands to run and they shouldn't take me long."

She walked away from him as he moved to the doorway to watch her, a sudden feeling of doom running through him. He looked back at the kitchen, waving at the staff and pointing to the door. Something was telling him to follow her and he could not shake the feeling that something was about to happen.

Larkin paused in front of a store, not really looking in the window, trying to remember what it was that she needed before she turned, not seeing the man who had been behind her. Her arm caught in his grasp, she was pulled towards an alleyway. She screamed and then struggled, pulling away from him and trying to run. She didn't hear Dave calling for her or see him running towards him.

The man spun, catching her again, dodging her flailing arms before suddenly shoving her towards a store window again and again until the window shattered and she fell through onto the tile floor in the little secondhand store, her body knocking the display flying. She landed among the debris and lay still, the customers standing in horror before the shop owner ran towards her as Dave shoved open the door and was on his knees beside her.

"Dave? What happened? Who is this?"

"A friend, Arly. Someone who has just been assaulted." He turned as he heard the sirens. "We'll need to clear your store. I'm sorry, but they'll have to go out the back door."

"Not a problem, Dave." The old man was on his feet, walking towards his customers and herding them towards the door at the back.

Dave's attention was on Larkin, assessing her even as he heard the paramedics coming towards him, asking what he had.

He drew a deep breath as he saw the spreading blood on her back, knowing somehow she had suffered lacerations. He shook his head as she was gently rolled to her side, neck brace in place and then onto the backboard. He stood, searching for the assailant, knowing he had disappeared.

Frankie was waiting as he exited the building, a frown in place.

"Dave? Who was that?"

"Larkin. She had been in her apartment and then said she had some errands. I felt I had to follow her."

"It's a good thing. I'll send someone for Tierney."

"Let me go. I think I should."

Frankie studied him for a moment and then nodded. "Go. I'll meet you at the hospital." He watched as Dave ran for the shop and his car, heading for Tierney.

Tierney stood in the open door, a hand on the door frame, the other on the wooden door, his eyes on Dave, shaking his head.

"No, that's not possible. She was only going to the apartment, she said, and then back here. She can't be hurt."

"I'm sorry, Tierney. She has been. And it was deliberate." Dave reached for the keys Tierney pulled out and stared at. "Come on. Let me lock up for you. Stay here." Dave walked back through the house, checking that it was locked up, knowing from Frankie that it was necessary.

Tierney almost ran into the Emergency Department, his footsteps loud on the tile. He slid to a halt and asked for Larkin, before he was told to have a seat. They would be with him shortly. He paced, knowing that he wanted to be back there, but he had to wait.

Dave paced with him, seeing Rylee heading his way. He stopped as she stepped into his hug, her voice quiet. She turned after a bit, heading for the chapel, knowing that was where she could best wait.

Caleb looked up as Frankie stopped in his office doorway, throwing down his pen and standing at the look on Frankie's face.

"Frankie? I don't like the look on your face." He walked towards him.

"It's not good, Caleb. Someone just tried to kill Larkin on the main street. From what we were told, the man tried to drag her into an alleyway. When she got away, he chased her and then kept slamming her into Arly's window until it broke and she went through it."

Caleb's face tightened as he moved towards the entrance of the building and a vehicle. Frankie followed, giving what details he knew about.

"Dave was there?"

"He was." Frankie confirmed that. "He said he had a feeling something was going to happen. He wasn't close enough to intervene and no one else did."

"That's our town? No one stepped in?"

Frankie shook his head. "There were only a couple of ladies there. One of them called it in."

Caleb sighed. "What is the world coming to?" He parked before they walked rapidly through the back entrance to the department, stopping to find out just where Larkin was. Frankie stood for a moment, watching as they worked on her, her face white, her clothing blood soaked, before he turned.

"I'll find Tierney. Dave was going for him. They should be here."

Caleb nodded. "Do that. Then come back here. We need to post a guard here. Who's free on patrol that can do that?"

"Aaron, I think. He's just starting his shift."

"Okay. I'll call for him."

Tierney looked up as he heard footsteps heading his way. Frankie sank down beside him, his hand on Tierney's shoulder for a moment.

"They haven't been out yet?"

Tierney shook his head. "Not yet. Did you see her, Frankie?"

"Just briefly. They're working on her." He pulled out his ever-present notebook. "Did she say where she was going this morning?"

"Just that she wanted to go to the apartment. We had taken all her personal stuff. She was worried about the furniture and wanted to talk to Dave about that. She had planned to be gone less than two hours, she thought, if that."

"Dave, did she talk to you?"

"She did, Frankie." Dave's eyes were on the people moving through the waiting room. "We agreed she'd leave the furniture for now. Rylee had left a box of goodies for her and she said she'd be back. I had this horrible feeling, Frankie, and that's why I followed her. I wasn't close enough to stop it."

Tierney had turned his head as Dave talked. "Dave, you never said what happened, just that I needed to come."

Dave shook his head. "I did, Tierney, but I don't think you heard me. Someone tried to take her away, she escaped and he shoved her through a shop window."

Tierney's face had grown paler as Dave spoke. "A window? How bad?"

"I don't know. She was bleeding, I can tell you that, but I wasn't the one treating her on site."

"Was she conscious?"

Dave shook his head. "No, she wasn't. And it's probably better that she wasn't, Tierney. She would have been in a lot of pain." He watched with concern as Tierney's body shook and his eyes closed briefly.

Frankie looked up as he heard footsteps approaching and touched Tierney's arm. Tierney jumped and looked up, rising as he saw the physician in front of him.

"Tierney? You're Larkin's husband?"

"I am. How is she?"

The physician pointed to his chair, taking the one Dave rose from. "Sit, Tierney. We need to talk." He drew a deep breath. It had been a long day already and it wasn't even half over for him. "She has a number of lacerations on her back, Tierney. One or two are deeper and we have a surgeon coming in to look at them. It's the blow to the head she took." He watched with compassion as Tierney's eyes slid closed. "We're going to do some imaging, X-Rays, what have you, just to make sure it's just a concussion and nothing more sinister. We'll come get you in a bit and you can go back with her." He rose, his eyes on Frankie, who stood as well and walked away with him.

"Doc?"

"She's lucky, Frankie. Find who did this. It was a vicious attack on her. I understand it was an attempted abduction gone wrong?"

"It would appear to be that. Let's get Tierney back to her as soon as we can. They need each other. I can't go into details, you understand, but Tierney's recovering from an abduction as well."

"What is it with you young people? Can't you find some other way to have excitement?" With that he walked away, leaving Frankie to smother a smile and shake his head.

## Chapter 20

Tierney finally stood at Larkin's stretcher, his hand on hers, the other hand gripping the rail. He watched her, willing her to awaken, but she didn't. He heard the movement around him but ignored it until his shoulder was touched. The surgeon stood there, a compassionate look on his face.

"Tierney, is it? This is your wife?" At Tierney's nod, the surgeon turned to study her. "We'll have to take her to the operating room, son. There are two lacerations we need to suture, and they're best done under anesthetic."

"Is it safe?"

"I could do it here. I'm waiting on the results of the imaging she had. That will determine how we proceed."

Tierney nodded, his eyes on Larkin's face, seeing the whiteness of it, the stillness, hearing the unspoken concern in the surgeon's voice. "I think I would rather you do it here, Doctor. If there's any chance there's more than a concussion, please, do it here. I don't think you can wait much longer, though, can you?"

The surgeon nodded, turning as the first physician walked towards him. "The imaging is clear. There is no fracture or bleeding." He watched as Tierney's eyes slid closed. "That's good news, Tierney. Now about those lacerations."

"We'll do them here, I think. Tierney has refused us permission to take her to the operating room and I'm fine with that. It was a precaution, more or less. Tierney, we'll need you to leave for a few minutes. The nurse will come get you when we're finished."

Tierney nodded before he reluctantly walked away. Lord, heal my lady. There is so much that I need to tell her and I haven't been able to. Heal her body, her mind, her soul.

An hour later, he paced beside the stretcher as Larkin was moved to a room. He heard a voice calling him and turned. Logan walked rapidly towards him, a frown on his face.

"Tierney? What are you doing here?" He looked past him. "Larkin? What happened?"

"Someone tried to abduct Larkin this morning. When that didn't work, he threw her through a store window."

"I heard about that." Logan's face showed his horror. "I didn't know it was her. How is she?"

"Concussion. She has lacerations on her back. I want whoever it was. They've taken enough from us." He turned and walked towards Larkin's room, leaving Logan staring after him.

Larkin's eyes fluttered open in the early morning hours, hearing muttering from Tierney and wondering how that could be. She reached for his hand, her touch stopping his muttering and bringing him awake and to his feet, his hand on her cheek.

"Larkin? Are you awake, my love?"

"I think so. Otherwise I don't want to sleep. This is a horrible nightmare. My head hurts. I can't see properly. And my back is stinging and burning and hurting. What did I go and do?" She was asleep again before he could answer.

Tierney turned as he heard the door and saw the man standing there, a dark shadow in the dim light, before the door swung closed and the man disappeared. He frowned, wondering who it was, before his attention went back to Larkin.

He watched as she slept, finally walking out to the waiting room, seeking what or who, he didn't know. He didn't see Abe and Murphy watching, having heard what happened. Larkin and Tierney had become dear to them, and they wanted to keep this couple safe.

Tierney turned as he heard footsteps and saw Logan walking towards him once more. He sighed. Now, how did he explain what happened?

"Tierney? Larkin? How is she?"

"She's asleep, Logan." He wavered as he turned to find a seat, Logan's hand out to steady him. "I'm sorry. I haven't slept and that doesn't go well with right now."

Logan frowned. "I still don't understand your connection to Larkin."

Tierney stared at him. "You have never heard? I had been held captive. Your cousins and Larkin were asked to come in and get me." He stopped, still puzzled by that. "I have no idea why. At the time, she was the only one who could calm me down. The rest is history, as they say."

"But I don't get what happened yesterday." Logan shifted in his seat, trying to watch Tierney's face.

"She had been abducted before we married. Yesterday, someone tried again. We can't understand why the window, though. That doesn't make a lot of sense."

"That's what happened? I didn't realize that. All I heard was that someone went through a window and then saw you here with Larkin."

"That's what happened. We have no idea who it was. Dave saw it happen but wasn't close enough to prevent." Tierney's head went back against the wall. "I'm sorry, Logan. I'm sorry she has chosen to take the way she has."

"I understand, more than you think." Logan dropped his head, a dark look covering his face for a moment. "I really didn't think we had been like that with her. She never said."

"She didn't think you would listen to her. That's what she told me." He looked at Logan for a moment. "I'm glad you were at our wedding. She didn't want anyone there, you know."

Logan nodded. "That's what Lincoln said. Mom and Dad still don't understand why."

"It's what she wanted. I will do almost anything to grant her wishes." Tierney sat for a few moments before he rose, his eyes on Logan. "Come with me, Logan. You can see her for a bit. Just be aware she has a concussion and there were lacerations they had to suture up on her back."

Logan nodded as he followed Tierney, pausing for a moment to pray for his sister. He hadn't realized how she had felt all these years, not until Lincoln had talked to him. He regretted that, knowing he could have done it differently with his sister over the years. He paused in the doorway, watching as Tierney stood for a moment beside the bed and then bent over Larkin, appearing to be talking to her.

Logan stood at the end of his sister's bed, watching her as she moved, his face tense and stern. He didn't want to be there, not seeing her like that, but he felt he had no choice.

Larkin's eyes caught movement around her and she frowned, not sure where she was. She heard Tierney's voice and turned that way.

"Tierney, where am I?"

"You're in the hospital, my love. You were hurt yesterday."

"I was? I don't remember." She tried to turn onto her back and stopped. "What did I do? And can I go home? I hate hospitals."

"I know you do. That's what you've told me. We'll get you home later this morning. We have to wait for the doctor." His hand traced her face, thankful that the glass had missed it.

"No, I want to go now." She squinted at the end of the bed. "Who's that?"

Logan moved up to stand beside her. "It's Logan, Larkin. I heard you were being difficult."

She sighed. "Is that what this is? I don't like it." She reached for his hand. "I'm sorry, Logan. I wasn't very nice to you, was I?"

"I should be apologizing to you. I didn't realize, Larkin, how you felt. I'm so sorry."

She nodded, her eyes closing against the pain. "You're welcome, Logan. Don't slam the door, please?"

Tierney choked back a laugh. She was definitely not making sense. He shot a look at Logan, and then smiled at the look on Logan's face.

"How be we call you tomorrow after she's home? Maybe, just maybe, she'll be making more sense."

Logan stared first at Tierney, then at Larkin. "Is she for real?"

Tierney snickered. "That's what I've been putting up with since they moved her up here. The concussion is playing games with her."

"I can see that." Logan paused, his eyes on his sister. "She will be okay, won't she?"

"She will be." Tierney sighed. "I guess we have to let Lincoln and your parents know."

Logan nodded. "I'll call them in the morning, although I have no idea how to explain it."

"Just say she had an accident. And warn them that I won't tolerate any interference in her care."

## Chapter 21

Cradling Larkin carefully in his arms, Tierney carried her into their home, setting her on her feet for a moment, before he turned, frowning as he saw Abe and Emma walking towards him. His attention back on Larkin, he studied her face, seeing the pain and fatigue there.

"Where do you want to be, my love?"

"Wherever you are. But I want a shower. I feel so dirty." She leaned against him, her eyes sliding closed for a moment.

Emma watched closely, before she looked up at Tierney. "Where's your bathroom, Tierney? The one with a shower."

"There's a guest suite here on the main floor." He picked Larkin up and carried her through to the suite. "There's just a shower, so that works." He set Larking down, watching to make sure she stayed steady on her feet. "Will you help her, Emma?"

"That's why we are here, Tierney. To help you in any way we can." She laid a hand on Larkin's arm. "Find us some clean clothes. And if you have a large T-shirt that is loose, it would be better."

He stared at her, lost in thought. "I do." He frowned. "Wait. I have a stool in the garage that would help. She could sit."

Abe's hand stopped his movements. "I'll get it. You find her clothes."

Tierney paced the office before he settled down to his work, being engrossed in it enough that he didn't hear Abe as he approached.

Abe watched for a moment before he spoke. "Tierney?"

Tierney jumped and then looked up. "Sorry, Abe. I forgot for a moment you were here. What was that you said?"

"I asked what I can do for you." He nodded at the pile of paper. "You should let Emma look through that."

"Emma? I don't understand." Tierney sat back, fatigue washing through him. He accepted the mug of coffee Abe handed him. "I'm sorry. I don't do no sleep very well anymore."

"Not when you're still recovering from your adventure, as we call it. As to Emma, you've heard of Trackers?"

"Who hasn't? They seem to be able to find anyone and anything." Tierney watched the smile cross Abe's face and his eyes narrowed. "What aren't you telling me, Abe?"

"Emma is Tracker. She set it up years ago." Abe nodded at the look on Tierney's face. "So, if you need help, she's willing."

"That would be great. I think I've found a clue but then Larkin was hurt." Tierney slumped back in his chair. "I talked to Frankie. He said they can't find her assailant. How far will it go?"

"I have no idea, Tierney. Whatever they want from you two, they seem willing to go to any length to get it from you."

"Larkin is starting to remember. She said she saw me with an older woman and a younger man in Hope. I don't remember them all that well. I was handed the manuscript, asked to authenticate it and then they left. It's just so strange. At the time, I was involved in another manuscript." He paused again. "Now, that's interesting."

Tierney was on his feet and to the filing cabinet, searching for the file he wanted. "Larkin has organized this for me. Thank goodness she did." He returned to his desk with file folders. "This is the information of the ones who asked me to do that manuscript. And this is the one that I was working on."

Abe reached for the folders, studying first the paperwork in one and then the other, a frown coming across his face. "There's a connection here, Tierney. I recognize some of the names from the second file." He looked up, compassion on his face. "They're not reputable people, but you would not have known that."

Tierney stared at him, horror crossing his face. "I did this to myself? And to Larkin?"

"Not necessarily. We would need to look into how they are related." Abe turned his head as he heard footsteps approaching and rose. "Emma?"

"Tierney, Larkin wants you." Emma was near tears and Abe knew that was a rarity with her. He simply reached to wrap her in his arms.

---

Tierney was on his feet and to the guest suite almost before Emma had stopped speaking. He hesitated at the door and then approached the bed, seeing how Emma had positioned rolled towels along Larkin's back. He sank to his knees beside the bed, his hand reaching out to lightly run down Larkin's hair.

Larkin roused, pain on her face, blinking at him. "You're safe, Tierney. I thought you were hurt or gone again."

"No, I'm right here. I don't plan on going anywhere. How are you feeling?"

She shrugged. "I don't know. I hurt all over. And I have a horrible headache."

"Did you get something for it?"

She shook her head. "I don't want anything. I don't like pain medications."

"If you need it, I would really like you to take it."

She sighed. "Let me think about that. Except it hurts to think." She studied his face. "Tierney, you didn't sleep. You need to."

"I will, my love. Abe's looking through some stuff for me. He said Emma would as well."

"Of course she will. She and Jace. She's Tracker, you know."

"So I hear." He watched as her eyes slid open and closed before they stayed closed. "Sleep, my love. I'll be in to awaken you in a couple of hours."

"I know." She sounded disgruntled for a moment. "I love you." Her voice died away as she slept.

Tierney's hand froze against her cheek, not quite sure he had heard correctly. He waited and then finally rose, heading for the kitchen and the coffee pot, knowing it was going to be a long day.

He dropped back into his chair, not quite sure what to do. Emma and Abe exchanged a look before Emma spoke.

"We don't want to intrude, and if you want us to leave, we will. But do you have a computer I can use? I think I know who these people are."

Tierney looked up and nodded towards Larkin's. "You can use that one. If you could solve this today, I would be grateful."

"I'm not sure I can solve it all, but I will give it my best shot. Whatever information I find goes to Frankie. He'll verify it and then go from there. It's how I work." She rose and seated herself at Larkin's desk, rapidly working through the security she had set up on her programs.

Abe watched for a moment, then came around to Tierney, pulling him to his feet. "Go, get some sleep, Tierney. You need to. Larkin's going to need you."

He nodded, almost asleep on his feet. "I know. I have to wake her in a couple of hours."

"We can do that. We're not going anywhere. Not today. You need us."

"But what about your son? Where's Isaac?"

"He's with my Aunt Peg. She's in her glory to have him there."

Tierney roused four hours later, glancing at his watch, and then rolling to his side, his eyes on Larkin. He suspected she had been roused but he hadn't heard them. He rose from the bed and walked around to her side, to drop to his knees, finding her waking.

She blinked at him, her vision clearer, and reached to touch him. "Tierney, are you okay? I dreamt you were gone again."

"No, I'm fine. You're the one who was hurt."

"I was? I don't remember. Is that why my back hurts?"

He nodded. "That and you have a concussion." He grinned suddenly. "Logan stopped by your hospital room real early this morning. You had him worried, you weren't making a lot of sense."

She shrugged and then groaned. "Tierney, can I sit up? I'm tired of laying down."

He helped her to sit on the side of the bed. "Can I check your back for a moment?"

She stared at him and then shrugged, flinching as he touched it. "How is it?"

"I can't tell. They bandaged the lacerations." He sat back on his heels. "Are you hungry? I can move you to the office and find something for you."

"Something light." She stopped as she heard footsteps heading their way. "Who's here?" He heard the fear in her voice.

"Abe and Emma are. Emma helped you to bed when we got home. They've been working on our mystery."

Emma stood in the doorway, a smile on her face. "Larkin, you are awake. Wonderful! I have some soup and tea for you. Where would you like it?"

"The office. I need to get to work."

"Sorry, Larkin. Tierney let me use your computer, and I'm in the middle of a search." She grinned at Larkin as she frowned at Tierney. "Tierney, I'm on the track of something that I think may well break your code."

He turned to look at her. "That would be wonderful. I want this over with now."

He stood and watched as Emma reached for the printer before handing him a sheaf of papers. "All this?"

"That's just for starters. I have searches running that will take a few hours. That material I will bring you tomorrow." Emma pointed at what he held. "Interesting people you have contact with."

"That do you mean?"

"I mean, there are forgers listed in there. I emailed a copy to Frankie. Hopefully, his team can find these people and soon."

"I won't plan on that." Tierney turned to watch Larkin, his eyes narrowed. "I don't want her hurt again. Not if I can avoid it."

## Chapter 22

Tierney paced the office later that day. Emma and Abe had left, promising to bring him anymore information she found. She had given the preliminary results and he had been shocked at who she had named. Larkin had nodded when she heard it, stating that of course that person would be involved. They had stared at her, but she had dozed off at that point. Tierney knew he needed to raise that with her again.

He sank down in his chair, his eyes on Larkin as she slept on the couch in the office. She had refused to go back to bed, telling him she needed to be near him. He smiled. Had she really meant it when she said she loved him? That would be something else to discuss with her at some point.

He turned back to the manuscript, searching through it, finally reaching the end of it. He sat back, staring at it, his fingers tapping against his chair arm. Emma was right, he thought. She had told him it was likely a link between the two of them that they hadn't found yet, other than what Larkin had remembered.

Tierney walked through the house, his thoughts dark, in the early evening. Who had done this, he wondered? He sighed as he heard the doorbell. We don't need this, he thought. Larkin is sleeping and she needs that sleep.

He stood, his eyes on the older couple who stood there, a frown on his face."

"Tierney? I don't think you remember me. I'm Larkin's father, Liam. We met when you were at her uncle's."

"Sorry, I don't remember a lot from those first few days." He stepped back. "Please, come in."

"Thank you. This is her mother, Leigh. Logan called us. How is she?"

Tierney could hear the worry in Liam's voice. "She's hurting. Right now, she's asleep again. I won't disturb her."

"We don't want you to." Leigh stood for a moment watching him before she reached to hug him. "Thank you, Tierney, for what you have done."

"What I have done?" Tierney was confused even as he pointed towards the kitchen. "Let's sit in there, if you don't mind."

He watched as they seated themselves before he asked if they wanted anything to drink or a meal. They both asked for coffee, shaking their head at food.

"Again, Tierney, we do want to thank you." Leigh shared a look with Liam. "We never realized how we were affecting her. It hurt to hear, but God was there in it. He let us know we can't go back over the past but we can change the future."

Tierney nodded. "No, we can't redo the past. And in the future, I won't tolerate her being hurt."

"We understand that, Tierney." Liam looked down for a moment before he asked. "That situation you were in. Has it been resolved?"

"No, it hasn't. We're working through that and what Larkin has been through. We think they're connected but we're not sure. She remembers seeing me with the couple who gave me the manuscript but not much more right now." He rose as he heard footsteps on the wooden floor. "Excuse me."

He stood in front of Larkin as she turned in the hall, watching her intently.

"Larkin?"

She spun and almost fell over. "I'm sorry, Tierney. I'm so sorry. I don't know what's wrong. I feel dizzy and uneven."

He grinned at her choice of words even as he reached to hug her. "It's the concussion, my love. That will do it. Now, do you want anything?"

She nodded. "Do we have juice? I can't remember."

"We do." He glanced over his shoulder at the kitchen. "And your parents are here."

"They are? Oh, no. They can't be. He'll go after them to."

His arm around her, Tierney led her towards the kitchen. "Who will go after them, my love?"

She stood for a moment staring at her parents before her mother was on her feet and standing in front of her.

"Larkin? I'm so sorry. I didn't know that was how you felt. Can you forgive your mother?"

Larkin drew a deep breath before tears sparkled in her eyes. "I can, Mom. I just wish it had been different."

Leigh hugged her daughter, holding on longer than she normally would. "I understand, you know. You never knew that I had to have this conversation with your grandmother, just like you did. Only it was when you were two. It should have been before that. I didn't realize I was copying her behaviour. Again, I am so sorry."

Liam swept his two ladies into a deep hug. "I'm sorry too, Larkin. I didn't realize how much my worrying about you had caused this rift. I can't go back, but I would like to try and change the future. I realize you're married now and that it is Tierney's right and privilege to worry about you. But you will always be my little girl. I can't change that I will worry about you."

"You should let God worry for you, Dad." She stepped back, finding Tierney there to sweep an arm around her and lead her to the table.

He set juice in front of her and reached for the soup in the fridge, heating some and setting it before her too. That earned him a frown that he only grinned at. Her parents were watching and exchanged a glance. Liam nodded. He had been worried that it would be a loveless marriage for the two, but he could tell the attraction was there. He saw the look of love in Tierney's eyes before he shuttered them. He knew Leigh and he would be talking later.

Liam rose after a while when Tierney nodded at him and followed him to the office.

"Where do you stand on the investigation?"

Tierney shrugged. "I have no idea. Frankie is not saying much, so I'm guessing he's not getting very far. A friend found a wealth of information for me today and passed that on to Frankie as well. I've been through the manuscript and made notes. I need to let them sit for a bit and think them over."

"Do you mind if I take a look?"

Tierney shook his head, handing him a copy of his notes. "Maybe you'll see something I missed. I just don't see the connection."

"Can I mark this?" At Tierney's nod, Liam's pen was out, marking, making notes, before he sat back, a frown on his face. He reached for the picture that Emma had somehow found. "I know this woman, but how?"

"You do? How?" Tierney looked up from his desk and then squinted at the clock. "I'll be back, Liam. I just need to see to Larkin."

Liam looked up, opened his mouth and then snapped it closed. No, they had to let him. As much as Leigh would want to be the one taking care of their daughter, she was married. That right no longer belonged to them.

Larkin looked up as Tierney laid a hand on her head and nodded. She was exhausted, but hadn't felt like moving. Her mother watched as Tierney swept her into his arms and carried her to the guest suite. He was not moving her upstairs tonight. He tucked her in, his hand resting on her as he prayed for her healing. Lord, I have no idea why this happened but You were there. She could have died but You protected her. Thank you.

He stooped to kiss her cheek as she slept, his quiet "I love you" echoing in her ear.

## Chapter 23

A week later, Larkin was healing. Her headaches had diminished and she was finally able to resume her work, amid complaints that she could have before. Tierney just shook his head, knowing how close it had been to losing her.

"Larkin? Do you remember anything else?"

"About what?" She looked up, her eyes on him. "About that couple? Or about when I saw you? You need to be more specific."

He began to laugh. "I can see that. First, about that couple. Emma has come up with names for them. Walter Lewis and Joyce Lewis. Mother and son, she says."

Larkin stared at him, her mind working. "Those names don't ring a bell. I think I knew them under another name. Now, what was it?"

She stared at him, her mind working before she nodded. "I know. Their names with William and Joan Lukas. That's it. I knew them from work. They had briefly been through the office one day. Was that a set up, do you think?"

"More than likely." He searched through the paperwork Emma had left. "I don't see that Emma found that name, but she likely did." He shot off a quick email to her, asking if she had.

He rose, reaching for her hand. "It's time to quit for the night. Tomorrow, we'll pick up everything. Maybe Emma will be in touch."

"Or Frankie will call to say he's solved it and arrested everyone involved." She paused. "Did you give those names to Frankie?"

"I did, my love. Now, dinner? What would you like?"

She shook her head. "I'm not real hungry tonight. Just a salad, I think."

"A salad it is."

Two hours later, he searched for her, finding her standing in the office, staring at her work.

"Tomorrow, my love. Come. The moon is rising and I would like to sit and cuddle with my wife."

She stared at him, shocked at his words. "You want to do what?"

"I'm courting you, my love. Isn't that what courting couples do?"

She shook her head at his grin. "I have no idea. I've never been courted before. But if you say so, I guess we must."

He slipped an arm around her, preventing her from leaning her healing back against the wicker of the love seat. He was content, he thought, even though they still faced unknown assailants and danger.

Conversation was quiet and sparse. They didn't need to talk, those two. Their hearts were talking to one another.

Tierney finally had to speak. "Larkin, what I am about to say? I don't mean any pressure on you. I just want to say I love you and want to spend the rest of our lives together. I have no idea if you love me."

She turned her head, watching his face in the dark, and reading her answer there. "I love you, too." She groaned. "Didn't I tell you that when I wasn't aware of what I was doing?"

"You did. I needed to hear it when you were lucid." He dodged the elbow she aimed at him. "We'll take it slow. We need to get whatever is hanging over us finished."

"That we do." She paused, a frown on her face. "Do you hear something?"

"I do." He shifted to rise, and stopped, feeling the weapon pressed to his neck.

They rose when ordered to do so, her hand reaching for his, until she was moved away from him. He struggled to reach her, a sudden blow sending him to the ground. Ordered to stand, he finally was able to, unsteady on his feet, his eyes on Larkin as they were shoved around the house and into a van. A commercial van, he thought, as he watched the roll-down door close and heard the snick of a lock.

He reached for Larkin, feeling around for her hand. She clutched at his, grasping it tightly. He could feel her shaking in fear. He damped down his own fear, trying to stay positive, but it was difficult. He had no idea who had them or why.

He listened closely but could hear little. He had no idea which way they were heading or if they were even still in Riverville. His head dropped to hers as she finally quieted. Lord, protect us. Keep us safe. Help us to escape.

———

## Chapter 24

Frankie looked up from his meal as he heard footsteps heading his way. Dave and Logan slid into the booth across from him. He searched their faces, his heart sinking.

"They're gone?"

Logan shook his head. "I have no idea. I tried to reach them, dropped by the house. There was no answer. The cars are there but the back door is unlocked. That's not them."

Frankie took a look at his meal and then rose, heading for the door, waving at Mac, the diner owner, as he did so. Dave and Logan were tight behind him.

Frankie walked through the house, not finding them. His heart sank. They were gone. Sometime yesterday they disappeared after Tierney had sent him that email.

He turned as he heard his name called and saw Caleb walking towards him.

"Frankie? They're not here?"

"No. It looks as if they've been taken again. Who is doing this?" He groaned as his phone chimed and he looked down at it. "Emma. She has more names for us and wants to meet." He looked around. "Actually, she's at the barricade, she says."

Caleb nodded. "Let me know what she has to say. I'm on my way to court this morning. I should be back in the office this afternoon. We need to find this couple, Frankie."

"I know we do. I'm afraid for their lives if we don't."

The techs shook their head as they approached. "We couldn't find anything, Frankie. Not a thing. There are mugs sitting outside on the patio. That's likely where they disappeared from."

"Thanks. Patrol officers are going door to door but I doubt we'll get much."

Emma handed Frankie the folder she had been holding when he finally found her. "They're missing. I tried to reach him last night but it went to voice mail."

Frankie nodded. "His phone is on his desk. So is Larkin's." He looked around, knowing that their abductors were likely watching. "What can you tell me?"

"Larkin remembered those names. I researched them. Nasty people, I must say. It doesn't surprise me Tierney went through what he did."

"And now, if they have him again, he'll have to go through it all again."

"Only, this time, it will be worse. Larkin's with him."

Frankie sighed. "You just had to mention that little point, didn't you? They'll use her against him and him against her."

He strode through the department building late that afternoon, tired and frustrated. They had no leads and he wanted them. The couple seemed to have just disappeared. Caleb looked up from his desk and beckoned him in.

"No word?"

Frankie shook his head. "No. No word. Not a sign of them. I don't get it."

"Was anything missing from his office?"

Frankie shook his head. "I can't tell. There was a manuscript on his desk, but I have no idea if it was the one he was working on. Emma might know." He sent off a quick text to her. He stared at her response. "That's the one, she said. He was going to talk to her today." He sighed. "Now what?"

"We keep looking. Any idea on a vehicle?"

"A neighbour saw a commercial type van parked down the road for a while late yesterday afternoon but didn't think much of it. There was no name on it."

"Of course, there wasn't." Caleb ran his hands through his hair, deep in thought. "We need to canvas everywhere we can. I know you've got that started."

"I have. I also need to speak with Logan and his family again."

Caleb nodded. "Let me know if I can be of assistance." He watched as Frankie walked away, concerned for his friend.

A week later, Frankie was frustrated. He had found no sign of the couple. No one had. That concerned him. Had they been taken somewhere else, Lord?

Then, word came about suspicious activities in some caves near the town. Frankie and Caleb looked at one another and then ran for their vehicles.

Doug Foster, a close friend and leader of the ETF squads, stood watching the activity around him. They had parked back far enough he didn't think they would be seen. He could see the tire tracks in and out and knew they were recent.

"Doug?"

Doug turned as he heard Caleb's voice. "Caleb? We getting ready to go in. I would suggest we go in and then patrol can go in after us, once we've cleared it."

Caleb nodded, knowing Doug would have weighed the situation and any action needed. "I don't have a good feeling, though. God is preparing us for something."

Doug agreed. "I know. I want my guys in and out as quickly as they can." He walked away, leading his men forward. He hesitated at the entrance, his eyes searching, before he turned.

"We need to move fast and be in and out as quickly as we can. I know these caves. There are some rooms off the main one but they don't go deep." He pointed to the sides and the men split up. He dropped his visor over his face and moved forward, hearing the sounds of the search over his com-link.

He reached the last room, his light shining around, before he heard Tom, his second-in-command, gave a cry and rush forward. His light dropped to find Larkin laying there, not moving.

"Is she alive, Tom?"

"She is but she's not in great shape. And what does she have on her ankles?"

"Shackles." Doug handed his weapon to Tom and reached to gather her into his arms. "Out. Now. I have a bad feeling." He could hear the chatter as his men rushed for the entrance, Doug and Tom on their heels.

They staggered as the blast that destroyed the caves sent shock waves towards them. They exchanged startled glances, knowing that they had just made it out. Doug's eyes dropped to Larkin and he ran towards the ambulance that was waiting.

Caleb was there, his eyes narrowing as he assessed her before he saw the shackles.

"Doug? Shackles?"

"Yeah. Shackles. She was on her own in there. Tom said it looked as if she was just dumped there. I didn't see any evidence of anyone else there where we found her."

Caleb could feel the anger growing inside him. "Has she not been through enough? And no sign of Tierney?"

Tom spoke up. "I talked to our guys, Caleb. One of the rooms looked as if someone else might have been there. Doug and I didn't go into that room."

Caleb nodded, his eyes on the ETF squad. "Take them in, Doug. We'll debrief there. This is going to hurt, you know." He looked around, feeling someone watching them. "Someone is out here. This was staged. It could very easily have taken your lives."

Doug frowned. "I don't think so. If whoever it wanted to do that, the bomb would have gone off when we were inside. It's like they wanted us to find her. But why?"

Caleb looked around, pointing to one of the patrol officers. "Did you ride with someone?" At her nod, he pointed to the ambulance. "In there. You're riding with her. She's under your protection. I'll have someone meet you there."

He watched as the paramedics worked on Larkin, reaching to take the shackles as they were cut off, a frown on his face. Who does this, he wondered? He knew Tierney's story and how they had found his shackles on him as well. Would the same be true? And just where was he?

## Chapter 25

Caleb stood for a moment in the waiting room of the Emergency Department of the hospital, his eye searching for someone, not seeing them there. He sighed. He had to send someone for Logan, then. And that meant Frankie. He turned as he heard Frankie's voice beside him.

"I've spoken with Logan. He and Aveleen are on their way in. He asked about Tierney."

"What did you say?"

"Just that he wasn't with her. I'm keeping as many details quiet as I can. I have spoken with each of the officers who were there and the paramedics as well." He looked around. "I don't like this, Caleb. Someone is here, watching. And the only people I see are townsfolk."

"I know, Frankie. That is disturbing." He pointed towards the exam rooms. "Come on. Let's find out what we can." He paused. "If Tierney's not here, who's her next of kin?"

Frankie shook his head. "I have no idea. I suspect her parents but we'll have to ask."

Caleb stood back, watching as the physician and nurses worked on Larkin. He frowned. Who had done this? Frankie was working through what Tierney and Emma had given him, but he wasn't really any further ahead than he had been. He looked up as the physician stopped beside him.

"How is she, Doc?"

"She's in distress. I can tell you that much. We're looking at pneumonia, I think, Caleb. She's lost weight since I saw her two weeks ago. What happened?"

"She was abducted along with Tierney. We found her today." Caleb shared a look with Frankie. "Has she been abused at all?"

The physician shook his head. "I see some bruises and scratches but nothing that I wouldn't have expected. What happened her ankles?"

"Shackles."

"Shackles? As in leg shackles? No wonder the flesh is rubbed raw. We can treat that. The lacerations on her back look good, all things considered. There's one we're watching that's inflamed. That could be feeding her fever."

"Who's her next of kin for treatment?"

The physician stopped. "Tierney's not here?"

Caleb shook his head. "We can't find him. He was abducted at the same time as she was. And we have idea why or where he is."

He looked at Caleb. "You're serious, aren't you?" He reached for the chart. "It says Tierney." He frowned as he looked up at Caleb. "And you're next on it, Caleb. Did you not know?"

Caleb stared at him. "No, I didn't. Now, why would she do that?"

"Because she was thinking ahead, knowing that if something happened, having you as next of kin would give you access to whatever you needed to without a court order. You will need a court order for formal records, but you can work with what you have now." He looked at Larkin and then back at Caleb. "Right now, we need to treat the laceration, the ankles and the suspected pneumonia. Here. Sign and we can get to it."

Caleb scrawled his name and then paused. "Her parents will expect to be the next of kin."

"That they will have to take up with her. Now, we can treat."

Caleb stood for a moment, his eyes on Larkin, a frown on his face before he turned to Frankie.

"Did you know?"

Frankie shook his head as the two men walked back towards the waiting room. "I didn't. But it makes sense you know." He sighed. "This is getting complicated, you know. I keep praying our friends will stop their adventures, but we keep getting sucked into another one."

"I know. I've usually been on the outside looking in. With Logan and now Larkin, I'm not. How do I explain this to Hannah?"

"I don't think you'll have to." Frankie nodded towards a chair. "She's waiting for you now. I suspect she was called in."

Caleb sighed again. "I suspect she was. Keep me updated, Frankie. I need to go talk to some people and I have no answers." He pointed towards Logan. "And how do I explain Larkin's actions to him?"

"God will give you the words. And it's not going to be a permanent thing, you know."

"I pray it isn't."

Logan stood as Caleb walked towards him, pausing to reach for Hannah's hands.

"Caleb? Is it Larkin?"

"It is, Logan. Let's sit."

Caleb sat, his legs stretched out for a moment. These chairs, he thought, are not made for someone as tall as he and his friends. He reached for Hannah's hand again, sharing a look with her.

"Caleb?" Aveleen's quiet voice caught his attention.

"Logan. Aveleen. We have Larkin. We do not have Tierney. We have no idea where he is. I can't go into many details, but she was found in caves just outside of town, within our patrol area. The ETF went in and brought her out." He paused, a bleak look crossing his face for a moment. "The physician doesn't think there's a lot wrong with Larkin. Bruising, some cuts, one laceration they need to address. They are concerned about pneumonia." He paused, drawing a deep breath. "The thing of it is was that she was wearing leg shackles when we found her."

Logan's face grew stern as he stared at Caleb. "Shackles? Like Tierney?"

Caleb nodded. "Just like him."

"Mom and Dad are on their way in. Who has to give consent if Tierney's not here?" Logan looked at Caleb as he made a sound. "Caleb?"

"For some reason, Larkin put me down after Tierney. That's something I will have to address with her."

"She did? That's bizarre. That doesn't sound like her at all."

Hannah spoke up. "Actually, Logan. It makes sense. We had had a conversation about next of kin one day. I know she was thinking through who to have. Nothing against you as her brother, but with what they're going through, this is likely a step she made knowing Caleb would agree."

"I think you're right, Hannah." Caleb looked up as he heard his name called and was on his feet and walking towards Frankie.

"Frankie? I don't like that look."

"I don't either. I just spoke to the county patrol. They found Liam and Leigh. They were heading this way and were run off the road. Bumps and bruises. The vehicle sounded like the van seen near Tierney's place."

"That's not what I wanted to hear. Why go after them?"

Frankie shrugged. "I have no idea." He looked behind Caleb. "Here comes Doc."

Caleb turned. "Doc?"

"We need to talk, Caleb, somewhere quiet." He pointed to the doors to the outside. "Let's walk. Frankie, you'll need to be in on this conversation."

The three men walked through the parking lot, the two officers waiting for the physician to speak.

Doc finally stopped, his face raised, his throat working as he swallowed hard.

"Larkin was awake for a bit. She's distraught to be it mildly. She says she was told Tierney had been killed. That's why they dumped her. They had no further use for her."

"She said that?" Caleb frowned. "We need to get Emma in to talk to her." He turned to Frankie. "We need to search, Frankie. I don't think he's dead. I think they wanted her to assume that."

"I know. I don't like it, Caleb. Let me talk to Abe about putting her with his guys."

## Chapter 26

Larkin turned from the window of the cabin she was assigned and frowned. This is no life, she thought. I know why they want me here, but I want to be free. This is not freedom. She stared down at her ankles, at the healing wounds and sighed. I can only imagine how Tierney felt, having them on for so many months.

Emma watched, knowing to a certain extent, how Larkin was feeling, having been told her husband was dead, but clinging to the very hope he wasn't. She approached Larkin, an arm coming around her to hug her tight.

"Emma? How did you ever do it? I mean, at the beginning."

Emma drew her down to the couch. "It was really hard. And I was really sick for a while. I had been drugged that first day and my uncle set it all up to prove that Abe was dead. Abe had been told I didn't want anything to do with him. God is the only hope I had. I didn't know if it was true or not. I prayed that it wasn't." She blinked back tears as she remembered. "But you, how did they tell you?"

Larkin stared at Emma. "You know, no one asked me that. I don't know if they think it's too soon or not. I mean, I've been home from the hospital now for what two days, three since they found me? Wouldn't they ask me that?"

"They should and they will. Frankie's sensitive that way. With you being sick, he wasn't pushing." She suddenly grinned. "Caleb was taken aback, you know."

"What do you mean?"

"You have him as your next of kin, after Tierney."

"No, that's not right. I didn't do that. I had Lincoln. So, who did that?"

"You didn't? Caleb couldn't figure it out. We need to tell him. Someone's been messing with your records, by the sounds of it."

Larkin nodded, her head dropping back on the couch as she slumped down. "Where is he, Emma?"

"I pray he's safe. Did they say what they wanted from you?"

"They think there is material that Tierney found that leads to a fortune in hidden treasure. I have no idea. He hasn't told me if he had. I know he talked to you."

"He did. He found some information, but he hadn't finished researching it when we left. Did he find more?"

"Probably. It would be on his desk." Larkin went to rise, but Emma's hand kept her in her place.

"Let me have your keys and tell me exactly where it is. Micah's are heading in to town for dinner. He can stop by and grab it for you."

"Thank you." Larkin grew quiet before she began to speak. She didn't hear Abe and Frankie enter, or notice Emma turn to look at them.

Larkin's eyes slid closed as she remembered that night. She remembered the feel of the man's arms as he drew her away from Tierney and then to the road where she and Tierney were shoved into a vehicle. She couldn't describe it much, other than it was a van for deliveries, she thought. She frowned. She remembered seeing a sticker on the side. It advertised milk delivery from One Man Dairy. That was strange, she thought. No one did milk deliveries anymore, did they?

Tierney had drawn her close to him, his hand on hers bringing her comfort. She didn't know how long they had driven around. She had finally slept, her head on his shoulder. She didn't feel the van stop or the door roll up. She didn't feel Tierney gather her to him and then awkwardly climb down from the van, into the dark.

She awoke the next morning, sitting up abruptly as she looked around. No, this wasn't home, she thought. Where am I? She turned, looking for Tierney but not seeing him. She jumped to her feet and tried to walk, tumbling to her knees as her feet tangled with one another and something pulled on them. She sat up, reaching for her feet in the half light of the room, the floor cold and damp under her. She realized it was a dirt floor, but that didn't explain why she couldn't walk.

She stared at the shackles she touched on her ankles and paled. Where was she? And who had done this? And just where was Tierney? She searched the crude room she was in and could find no way out other than the door and she had tried that. It was locked.

She stood for a moment, looking around, finally seeing the bottles of water sitting on a table near the door. She was hesitant to drink them, but she needed water. That much she knew.

How long it had been before someone unlocked the door and beckoned her out she had no idea. She stood for a moment, staring at the man, a frown on her face. She knew him, she thought, just not from where. When she didn't move forward, he walked towards her, grabbing her arm and forcing her from the room and to another room where she was shoved down into a chair. She blinked at the sudden light, realizing it was late afternoon by then. It could only have been one day since they were taken, she decided.

She heard shuffling behind her and spun, despite the man's hand on her shoulder. Tierney looked up at her and nodded. She froze, seeing him in shackles once more. He shook his head at her, trying to convey his love in his glance.

He was forced into a chair beside her and told not to look at her. She was forced to turn her head back to look forward. She heard the questions hurled at Tierney, but didn't hear his responses. Then, she realized, he wasn't responding. And just why was that, she wondered?

She was finally shoved back into her room. She dropped to her knees and then spun, staring at the door. No, they hadn't brought a meal, now had they? She searched through the darkness, not finding anything but the bottles of water. How long, Lord, she cried? How long will we be here? How long until we die? Do You even care?

---

159

This went on for four more days. She could tell Tierney was having trouble functioning and she just didn't know why. She couldn't see any bruising or cuts on him, so what was wrong?

After about a week, she was pulled from her room. She had trouble focusing by now herself, given the lack of nourishment. She stumbled as she walked, the shackles clanking together and pulling on her ankles. She was surprised when she was walked outside and then shoved into a vehicle. Not the same one, she thought. Now, where am I going? Lord, I hope You know.

She could not see where they were heading but she knew it wasn't in town. When the vehicle finally stopped, she was pulled from it and then shoved towards a cave. She tried to fight herself free but couldn't. She was shoved hard, through the caves, until she reached the last area, and then shoved to the floor, her head hitting hard. Her vision darkened and she was lost to consciousness. She didn't hear the footsteps retreating, didn't hear the conversation about a bomb. She didn't hear, anything.

She looked up at Emma when she finished, tears sparkling in her eyes. "Where is Tierney, Emma? He told me he loved me that night, just before we were taken. I can't lose him. Not like this. Not yet."

Emma reached to hug her, Larkin clinging to her. "We'll find him for you, Larkin. That I promise." Emma looked over Larkin's head at Abe and Frankie, who had sat, stern looks on their faces as Larkin talked, knowing if they moved, she might stop and not start again.

"Did you see anything when you were put in the vehicle, Larkin?" Emma's voice was quiet as she spoke.

"No. I don't think so. Wait. I did. We were outside of town. There was an old tower there. Something like an old fire tower. I can't be sure though. I'm sorry."

# Chapter 27

Frankie moved so that he was closer to Larkin, bringing her eyes to him. She sighed. *He had been there, hadn't he, Lord? Well, I guess that's good. I don't have to repeat myself. At least, I hope I don't.*

"Larkin? Can you describe the people at all?"

She shook her head. "Not really. I wasn't allowed to look at them. Other than the man who would bring me back and forth from my room. Him, I know him. I just can't think where." Her voice stopped as she thought through where she had seen him. "I've seen him in town. At the diner. At church." She looked up. "He's from the church. I just don't know his name."

"That's okay, Larkin. I'll have a police artist work with you on a sketch, if you will." Frankie looked down at his notes. "Now, this tower. We have one about three miles from here. Just inside the town boundary. Would that be it?"

She shrugged. "I've never seen that one, so I don't know." She looked at Abe as he handed her his phone and then stood back. She frowned at the photo he had pulled up. "This is it, I think. I really don't know. I wasn't paying much attention to what was going on, you understand."

"We know, Larkin. We know." Frankie paused, his eyes on Emma. "I'm going to head in and see what I can find. You've done good, Larkin. We'll find Tierney for you."

"Dead or alive?" Larkin shoved away from the couch, her feet flying as she ran for the bedroom, shutting the door quietly behind her before she threw herself on the bed, her eyes staring at the window, her heart hurting.

Emma watched her go, her thoughts chaotic for a moment. "Do you have a name, Frankie, that you didn't say?"

"I do. Try Eb Lake."

Abe stared at him. "Eb?"

Frankie nodded. "We've been hearing rumours about him lately. I haven't been able to track him down to talk to him about another case I'm working on."

Emma spun, heading for the door. "I'll be back. I want my laptop. She can't be left on her own." She spun back towards Abe. "How safe will she be here? You know we've been attacked here before."

"I know, Emma. We may need to move her to the house. There's the safe room there as well as the tunnel."

"That is likely what we'll do. I fear for her, Abe. It's coming to a head and that increases her danger."

Abe nodded as he watched Emma run for their home, before he turned to Frankie.

"What can we do?"

"Keep her safe. They'll try to get to her again. I just don't get why they dumped her like that."

"Tierney." When Frankie looked at Abe, he repeated himself. "Tierney. Use her as a threat against him to make him do what they want. Only I don't think it will."

"I pray we find him soon."

Two days later, Larkin paced the cabin, her eyes on the door. She needed to get out, only she had no where she could go. She had no transportation. She sighed. Now what, Lord? Are you trying to get my attention? Because if You are, You have it.

She turned at the tap on her door and pulled it open, frowning. Abe stood there, a grin on his face.

"Come on, Larkin. Grab your shoes, your purse, whatever you need. We're breaking you free for a few hours."

"You are?" She ran for her purse, shoving her feet into her shoes, and then pulling the door closed behind her. "Where?"

"To town." Abe pointed at his vehicle. "Emma has called. She needs you to come to her office. We think we've found the man responsible for part of what you've been through."

She stared at him, her hand pausing on her seatbelt, before she clicked it close. Lord, will this find Tierney? I need him home. He would tell me I've been strong, but I'm breaking up inside.

Abe walked Larkin into Tracker's and then back to where Emma was standing.

"Larkin? You're okay?"

Larkin shrugged. "I have no idea how I'm supposed to be." She looked at Emma with hope in her eyes. "You have news?"

"Not what you wanted. I haven't found him. But I found the woman and the younger man." She pointed at a chair in her office, waiting until Larkin had perched on the edge of the seat before she sat in her own chair. "I have given the information to Frankie but I did want to talk to you about them." She hesitated, not quite sure what to say. "They have been seen in town and also in Oak City. The authorities are looking to find them, but haven't yet."

Larkin sat back, frustration evident. "So, we're not really any further ahead. How long will it take, Emma, until Tierney's either home or dead for real?"

Emma shook her head. "I know you're frustrated. We are too. I can't tell you how frustrated I was for ten years, thinking Abe was dead, until he walked into this very office, thinking he would ask Tracker to find me."

"And there you were."

"That's right. We're working as hard as we can, Larkin. You have to know that." Emma watched as Larkin fought for control of her emotions, fighting back her tears.

"I know you are. I don't blame you. I blame whoever it is." She pointed to the manuscript Emma had borrowed. "Did you find anything else in there?"

"Actually not yet. Tierney is very thorough in his work. He has documented everything that he could find and Jace, who works for me, is working through it. He hasn't said if he's found anything. I have also asked another friend to help search."

Larkin sighed and then rose. "Thank you, Emma. I appreciate all you've done." She turned to Abe. "Abe, I'd like to go back to my own home. I need that."

Abe nodded. "We suspected that you would. Come on, then. First a meal at the diner and then we'll take you home."

*Chapter 28*

Three more weeks had passed. Larkin had taken to pacing all night, sleeping in fits and starts during the day. She grew pale and lost weight. Her family tried to get her to move back with them but she refused. They looked in askance as her as she stood up to them, something she had never done. Having Tierney in her life and with him validating her choice to live her own life, supporting her in her decisions, he had given her the strength she needed to tell her family that she was an adult and that she could and would make her own decisions.

Lincoln silently applauded her, confiding in Holly that he was glad she was taking a harder stand with them. And that it was about time. Logan was still not sure how he felt, given that his little sister was still in danger.

She turned as she heard her name called after church one Sunday. She frowned at the man before she recognized him.

"Micah?"

"That would be me." He grinned at her. "Kat wonders if you would like to join us for a meal."

She studied him before looking at the young woman approaching. "I don't eat much and I'm not great company."

"That's okay. We had our own adventure, so we completely understand."

"You did?" She shook her head. "No way!"

---

167

"Actually, all of Abe's men did." Kataleen smiled at her. "And it's okay to be down and discouraged. We've all been there, but other than Emma, we really don't know how you feel. Not like this." She reached to hug Larkin. "If you want, we'll do lunch. Or if you prefer, we'll just come spend time with you."

Larkin stared at first Kataleen and then Micah. "You would do that? Just spend time with me?"

"We would, Larkin. We would like to do that. Even if you don't want to talk, we can be there with you." Micah watched the emotions flickering over her face before she finally nodded.

"Okay, then. I'll meet you at my home."

Micah's hand on her arm stopped her. "Did you walk or drive?"

She glared at him for a moment before her face softened. "I walked. I have this fear of vehicles right now. Especially if I'm on my own."

He pointed to his truck. "Hop on in, Larkin. If we're heading to the same place, no point in you walking." As Larkin settled herself, she didn't see the look Micah exchanged with Abe, who waved and then walked towards the rest of his men. Micah had been asked to stay with Larkin and Kat had been asked as well. Abe had a lead on where Tierney was and didn't want Larkin on her own. Micah prayed that this lead would work out this time, that the Lord would let them find Tierney and bring him home. Abe had talked to both Frankie and Caleb about the rumour. They had decided Abe would check out the building and if needed, call in help.

Larkin finally turned on Micah, her eyes narrowed. "Micah, it's late afternoon. There is no way you're staying here just to spend time with me. Give. What's the real reason?"

Kat began to laugh as Micah shook his head. "Larkin, what Micah couldn't tell you is that Abe had a lead on where Tierney may be. We're just waiting to see if it was true."

Larkin spun, hope on her face. "Is that true? Dear Lord, please! Bring him home!"

Micah excused himself as his phone vibrated. He turned to stare at Larkin as he listened, his eyes sliding closed.

Larkin was watching him and her heart sank as she saw that. Please, Dear Lord, please! I don't ask for much. Just bring Tierney home to me. That's all I want.

Kat approached Larkin, her arm going around her, as she watched Micah walk back towards them.

"Micah?"

"Larkin, that was Abe." He swallowed past the lump in his throatl, his eyes closing for a moment. "They have Tierney. They found him. He's on his way home."

"They found him? He's coming home? He's alive?"

"He's alive, Larkin, and insisting on coming here. Matt has called in a physician friend to meet them here." Micah's hand went out to steady her. "God has been good, Larkin. He kept Tierney alive for you."

She nodded before she turned and walked away from them, heading for the stairs and her bedroom. She sank to the bed, her face buried in her hands.

Lord, I doubted. I doubted You would bring him home but You are. I have no idea what we're facing together or if the ones responsible have been caught, but please, Dear Lord, help us.

She finally rose, heading for Tierney's bedroom and then turned. No, she thought, the guest suite. That would likely be best. Quickly gathering clothes for him, she ran for the stairs and down them, stopping for a moment in the kitchen to watch Kat as she prepared food for the men.

"I'm sorry, Larkin. I should have asked." Kat stared at the sandwiches she had made.

"I don't mind, Kat. You needed something to do and I wasn't thinking of that." She turned, heading for the bedroom, pausing in the office for a moment, before she turned to find Micah.

"Micah? Didn't you say you did research for Abe? And that Kat researches family trees?"

"We do. Why?"

"Because I want you to talk to Emma. Take a look at the manuscript she has and see if you or Kat can come up with something. Anything." She turned before he could answer, her mind already looking ahead to what she needed to do.

Micah nodded. "She has already asked me to do that. Kat as well. We've found some interesting items, but we needed to talk to Tierney about them. Now, we can." He reached for the clothes she held.

"Here, let me. Is there anything you needed to do in the room?"

She paused in the bedroom doorway, looking around before moving to the bed and pulling back the covers and then heading for the bathroom. She found towels and laid them out, not sure if they would be needed right away. She turned to Micah, finding him studying her intently.

"Micah?"

"You remind me of someone, Larkin, and I'm not sure who. It will come to me."

"If this person is the one they're really after, please find her and let them know they have the wrong person." He grinned at her grumpy-sounding reply. "Now, there's a stool in the garage. Can you find it for me and bring it in? That way, it's here if Tierney needs it." She pointed to the shower. "This is hard, Micah. I have no idea how he is or what he's been through." She paused again in her speech, tears sparkling briefly in her eyes before she fought them back. "This is the second time for this. I want this over, now."

"We know you do. We're working towards that for you." Micah disappeared, returning in a few moments with the stool, setting it inside the bathroom door, before he stopped beside Larkin, a hand on her shoulder as he prayed for her.

# Chapter 29

Standing just inside the open front door, Larkin wrapped her arms around her middle, watching as the vehicles pulled to a stop in the driveway, hope and fear running through her. The men exited, two or three of them, and she wasn't sure of their names, walking around the house. She knew what they were doing, just didn't want to admit it to herself.

She watched as Abe opened the back door of his SUV, standing for a moment, his eyes raised to meet hers as he nodded and gave her a smile. She sighed. Tierney was home. Thank you, Lord. Now, we just have to heal him, don't we?

Abe helped Tierney slide from the vehicle, his hand steadying him as his feet hit the ground and he stood, swaying a bit before he nodded. Matt reached for him as well. His arms draped across their shoulders, the two men supported Tierney as he walked towards the house, their own arms around his back. Tierney stopped at the stairs, staring at them, knowing he had to walk up them and not sure if he even could. Matt and Abe exchanged a look before Tierney raised a shaking leg and set his foot on the bottom step, drawing in a deep breath as he did so. Inching his way slowly upwards, he stopped at the top of the stairs, swaying again, the only thing keeping him from falling backwards the arms supporting him. He then inched towards the door, determination to succeed on his face, his eyes finally raising, searching for Larkin.

Once inside the door, he stopped, his breathing heavy, his whole body shaking from the effort but he refused to collapse. His eyes searched again, finding Larkin watching him, her hands covering her mouth, tears she didn't know she was shedding sparkling on her cheeks. She moved towards him and then was in his arms, hers tight around him, his holding her as close as he could. She finally stepped back enough she could look at him, seeing the strain of the last four weeks in his face, the fatigue, the black circles under his eyes, the lost look in his eyes, defeat and almost shame in his bearing. She looked around him at Matt, who moved forward, a hand going under Tierney's arm to steady him.

"This way, Tierney. Larkin, you have a room ready for him?"

She slipped an arm around Tierney, sliding under his to do so. "The suite down here. It's ready for him." She looked up at Tierney, watching carefully as he swayed, his feet stumbling over one another. "I left towels in the bathroom, but I don't think he'll manage even a shower."

"Not right now, Larkin. Let me get him settled." Matt turned as he heard footsteps behind him. "Here's John and Mary. Do you know them from church?"

Larkin peeked back over her shoulder. "No. I don't think I've met them. I mean, I've seen them there."

"John's a physician and his wife is a nurse. She'll stay with you for a few days, I suspect."

173

"I can't ask them to do that." Larkin felt herself beginning to panic and becoming overwhelmed, not feeling the confident person that her family knew her to be.

"They do this, Larkin. It's part of their ministry, to serve like this." Matt shared a look with John. "How be you go with Mary for a moment? We'll let you back in as soon as we get him settled." He helped Tierney to sit on the bed.

Tierney reached for Larkin, pulling her down beside him. "It's okay, my love. Matt's right. Let me get settled and then you can come back." He stared at his hand. "I'm just so dirty, Matt. I don't want to crawl into those sheets."

Matt watched Larkin walk away, her head turned to watch Tierney before he spoke. "John, do you think we can get him in and out of the shower?"

Feeling clean once more, Tierney sank gratefully down under the blankets, not seeing John's frown or his look at Matt.

"Where did you find him, Matt?"

Matt shook his head. "We have to talk to Frankie yet, so we can't say much. But it wasn't a nice place. I'm surprised he's still alive." He looked towards the door, knowing he needed to go find Larkin, but he had to talk to John first. "He told us they tried to convince him Larkin was dead. From what he said, their treatment was brutal. He'll need our prayers, for sure."

"That goes without saying. Now, let's look him over and see what we need to do for him."

Thirty minutes later, John watched as Larkin hovered in the doorway, not sure if she should enter but not willing to walk away. She finally approached the bed, sinking down to sit beside Tierney, her hand resting on his face, stilling his movements before his eyes flickered open and closed. She studied the IV line that ran to his hand before she looked up at John.

John watched for a moment, a frown on his face. "She has that touch, doesn't she?"

Matt nodded. "I had heard she did. So does her brother, Logan. And I hear Lincoln's wife has it."

Larkin turned, her eyes on Matt. "Did you find them?"

"No. We didn't. They had to have heard we were coming, but I have no idea how."

"They're watching you. That's how. They knew I had been at the compound, then moved home. I know they're watching. I've seen signs in the back yard."

"You've seen signs and you haven't told us?" Frankie's voice came from the doorway.

Larkin was on her feet, her eyes flashing with sudden anger. "Yes. There were signs. But what good would it have done to have told you? They weren't there. You wouldn't have found anything, now would you?" She turned to Matt. "Matt, can we please clear the room? I'm sorry, John. I don't mean to offend you. I need to talk to you with just Tierney here."

"That we can do, Larkin. You can talk to the others in a bit." He nodded at Frankie, who frowned and then turned and walked away, frustration evident.

Larkin watched at John closed the door and then stood, back to it, his eyes on her. Lord, this lady is hurting in ways I can't even begin imagine. Heal her heart. This hurt goes back a long way, I think.

"John, how is he? Really?" Larkins' voice was quiet as she sank back to the bed, her hand reaching to touch Tierney's chest above his heart.

"He's dehydrated, Larkin. What else he has suffered and how it affected him, I won't know until I can talk to him. He's had it rough."

"I know he has. I saw him the first time this happened. He was unconscious when we went in to get him."

"The first time? This has happened before?" John pulled a chair over and sat, his eyes on Larkin, his heart breaking for the young couple.

Larkin nodded, her thoughts jumbled. "My cousins and I were asked to go in and bring him out. We haven't been able to track who it was exactly that asked that. Anyway, it was in a crude prison. He almost didn't make it." She raised her eyes to him. "So, how does this affect what he suffered before? He was still recovering from that. He was gone for two months or so the first time."

John shook his head, not quite sure what to think. "I don't know, Larkin, to be honest with you. I really need to take him in to the hospital and do testing."

Larkin shook her head. "If we can avoid that, I would like to."

John sighed. "We'll do what testing we can. Mary drew blood for me and I'll drop it off at the lab today. We need to rehydrate him." He paused, not quite sure how to phrase what he needed to say.

"You think he'll suffer from post traumatic stress, don't you? I would expect him to. How do we deal with that?"

"That we can work with. We need to get him well and on his feet again. We also need to get you back to your full health."

She shook her head. "It doesn't matter about me. Just Tierney. He needs to get well." She turned to look at him and John caught a glimpse of someone else for a moment.

"Larkin?" When she turned to look at him, he questioned her. "Do you have a sister? No? Female cousins?"

"No. I am the only female in the family. Dad was an only child. Mom's sister didn't have any children. Her brother had two boys. They're the ones that I went in with to find Tierney." She sat back, not realizing that Frankie had opened the door again and stood there at John's nod. "I still don't get it. Why were we asked to go in? It's not what we do. The boys teach. I'm a secretary."

Frankie spoke, causing Larkin to jump and then spin to stare at him. "That's what we're working on, Larkin. It appears you have a double or someone made to look enough like you to pass for you. Have you had any problems in the past?"

She shook her head. "None. I mean, you always have issues of one kind or another but nothing I can put my finger on." She turned to study Tierney. "I just would hate it if I were the cause of his

177

problems. And I don't know that I'm not." She looked at John before looking at Frankie. "I need to know, Frankie. How do we find out?"

He nodded. "I have a detective working on that. And Emma is as well." He turned to look behind him for a moment. "Emma's here now, Larkin. Can you come talk with her?"

## Chapter 30

Larkin stood for a moment, her eyes on Emma, before she walked towards where she stood in the living room, looking out the front window.

"Emma?"

Emma turned, reaching to hug Larkin. "I'm so glad Tierney's home. How are you now?"

Larkin shrugged. "I have no idea. I mean, I'm so glad he's home, but he looks awful, Emma. He needs to heal and he can't if we don't find out who it is."

Emma nodded, then looked around. "Is there somewhere we can talk?"

Larkin turned, heading for the office. "In here. Why?"

"Because I want to talk to you in private. It's necessary. The guys wouldn't say a word, but you need to hear this first. I should be talking to Tierney but I can't."

"What did you find?" When Emma didn't answer, just walked around the room, Larkin began to shake. "You're scaring me, Emma. Please? What did you find?"

Emma spun, walked towards Tierney's desk and pointed at the manuscript. "The manuscript? It's a forgery, I believe. I think that's what Tierney had discovered. Why he was taken, we don't know. He may be able to explain it, but I would not be surprised if he didn't know."

"How do you know it's a forgery?"

"I had the paper tested in a lab. It came back as modern paper and ink that had been doctored to look old." Emma's hand rested on the manuscript.

Larkin frowned as she watched Emma's movements. "I guessed that. But what is in it?"

"That's what we are still working on. I think Tierney has ideas that he hasn't shared yet."

Larkin walked to the desk, bending so she could study the edges of the pile of the manuscript. "Emma? What's this? What's on the edges? I don't think that's supposed to be there."

"What? What are you seeing?" Emma reached for the manuscript, her eyes narrowed as she rotated it. "You're right. There is something there. We needed the right light to see it." She looked around.

"What do you need, Emma?"

"A camera. I don't have mine."

Larkin was away and then back quickly, her bare feet skiffing across the wood floor, reaching out her hand. Emma took the camera, glancing at it, and then taking a good look.

"This is a professional camera, Larkin."

"I know. I wanted to start taking portraits of animals and invested in it. I would rather work with animals than people. Am I strange?" She gave a self-deprecating laugh.

Emma began to laugh. "I don't think so. You need to get that Sheltie pup you had your eye on."

"She'll have been sold."

Emma shook her head. "No, she's not. My friend held on to her at my request. Abe and I would like to give you the puppy."

"Oh, I can't let you do that!" Larkin shook her head. "I can't. It's too much."

"No, not really. The friend won't charge me for her. She's already said that. She knows your story and understands."

Larkin drew a deep breath. "I'll think on it. That's something Tierney and I need to discuss. If we ever can."

"You will. And with the personality of this pup, she'll bring comfort to you both. Now, what do we have on this paper?"

Emma began to shoot her photos, not seeing Frankie walking towards them.

"Emma? What are you doing?"

She looked up for a moment, her concentration still on her task. "Larkin discovered markings on the edge of the manuscript. We needed the right light and had it today." She stood back, her focus on the photos on the camera. "I think we've done it, Larkin. Let me borrow your memory card and I'll download them. Frankie, your team will need these." She frowned, turning first to study Larkin and then Frankie. "Larkin, have you had any threats, odd packages, anything?"

Larkin shook her head. "No, not recently. Tierney didn't say that he had either before we married. Why? Should we have? Isn't that the way it goes?"

Frankie grinned for a moment, before he sobered. "It's usually how it goes, Larkin, but you two are different. We've never had someone shackled and kept in a prison cell like Tierney has been. Not once, mind you, but twice."

"I can't understand that, Frankie. Why shackle him? And keeping him in a jail cell? When the boys and I went in to find him the first time, there were no guards. We could hear movement in other cells, I think three or four, but I can't be sure. And just why were the boys asked to go in? And me? It's not what we do. Unless we were and still are being set up for something. I don't know if the company that contacted the boys even exists." She turned at a sound from Emma, meeting her compassionate glance. "Emma? You searched, didn't you?"

"I did, Larkin. I'm sorry. That company doesn't exist. It's a dummy company set up likely just for that particular event. And the phone number and email no longer exist. We can't find them any way we look."

Larkin nodded before she sighed, her eyes on Frankie. "That's what you were going to say?"

"Part of what I needed to talk to you about. But there is something else. Micah asked me if we had looked for someone who could be your double."

"He mentioned I looked like someone. That's something Tierney and I have discussed, that we were targeted by mistake. He doesn't think it was him, but he thinks I might have been. How do we find out? And don't tell me we have to find her first before we're sure." She sounded grumpy once more and sighed. "I'm sorry. This has not been that great few weeks."

"No, it hasn't, Larkin. And I really do understand. Deirdre and I had our own adventure before we married." He nodded at her look. "Now, about your double. We have reports from town that someone looking like you has been seen around one of the bed and breakfasts. I have detectives heading that way now to see if they can find her."

"I pray you do and that she's been the one all along." Larkin turned and walked away, leaving Frankie staring after her, his mouth open to speak.

Emma laughed, delighted that Frankie was at a loss for words. "You needed to talk to her, still? Somehow, I think you'll have to wait." She perched on the desk behind her. "What have you found that you can share? Abe is worried, more worried than I have seen him in a while."

Frankie nodded. "We are all, Emma. There's something we're missing and none of us can figure it out." He pointed to the memory stick she held. "Unless what you just took in pictures helps."

"It might. I'll need to download them and work on finding out what it is. Numbers and letters." Her voice slowed as she looked at the stick and then up at Frankie. "Account numbers?"

Frankie sighed. "I suspect so. We just need to determine who and where."

## Chapter 31

During the early morning hours, Matt ran for Tierney's room, hearing the shouts and disturbance coming from there. He reached to try and hold Tierney still, fighting with the flailing arms and twisting body without much success. John reached to help, his head turning to call for Mary and for her to bring the sedative he had ready. Neither man heard the scurrying footsteps as Larkin flew into the room, her eyes huge with worry, a tortured look on her face. She was in and under Matt's arm, on her knees by the bed, an arm around Tierney, her other hand over his heart, soft murmurings coming from her that the men could not understand.

Matt watched in amazement and finally stood back, his hands stuck in his pockets, as he watched Tierney's frenetic movements slow and then still as his eyes flickered open and shut before they stayed open. He watched as Tierney's gaze searched the room before he found Larkin beside him.

Tierney reached to touch her face, a sigh coming from him. "You are alive. They tried to tell me you were dead. I didn't believe them." He stopped for a moment. "They said you weren't the one they wanted. That's why you disappeared. That someone else is who they want. They told me I know her. But I don't."

Larkin nodded, unable to speak for a moment. "That's what Frankie has discovered. That I am not who they want. They are trying to find her." She looked past him for a moment, a frown on her face. "But I don't understand why they want you."

"There's something in that manuscript. I have been able to determine towns and countries from a code. But I'm not sure what it relates to."

"I found numbers and letters around the edge of it yesterday, I guess it is by now. Emma took photos. Is this what they want?"

Tierney nodded. "That's what they kept asking for. Account numbers. I have no idea where they belong to." His eyes slid closed as his breathing deepened and he slept. Larkin stayed kneeling beside him, afraid to move, afraid if she did, he start having nightmares again. She only knew that her touch had calmed him and brought him back from the darkness he had been in.

John had watched, eyes narrowed, as Larkin had calmed Tierney. He looked up, seeking an answer from God, but none came. He just had to accept that was how it was.

Matt reached for Larkin and drew her to her feet, shaking his head as she tried to pull away from him.

"Come on, Larkin. We need you to sleep too. He'll need you in the morning. You need your rest."

She slumped down on the couch, her brows lowered, a frown in place as she stared past Matt at the hallway. "Why him, Matt? Why him?"

Matt seated himself on the coffee table, head tilted to watch her. "What do you mean?"

"I mean, why him? Why did they choose him to look at the manuscript? There are others less reputable that would have gladly looked at it."

Matt nodded, understanding what she was asking. "I don't know. I don't think any of us know yet." He reached for his phone, glancing at the text message. "Abe is on his way in. That's strange."

"Why would he be coming in at this time of the morning?" She squinted at the clock in the low light she had on in the living room. "It's only two."

"He's either found out something or someone has threatened either you or Tierney. I would suspect the latter."

Larkin nodded. "I just don't understand, Matt. Why is God allowing this? We are believers. We do what we're supposed to. So, why?"

"That's a question I'm not sure even how to begin to answer, Larkin. Greg would be the one to talk to."

She shook her head. "No, I don't want to talk to him. I don't want a long-winded explanation. What are your thoughts?"

"Murphy would say that God had a plan and purpose we don't know about yet. I suspect that is the truth." He studied the young woman in front of him, not quite sure how to respond. "Why are you asking?"

"What do you mean? Of course I'd ask something like this. Wouldn't you?"

Matt gave a grin. "I guess both Sarah and I did at some point."

Larkin pointed at him. "You need to go home and now, Matt. John's here. You need to be with Sarah."

He shrugged. "I can stay. Abe would ask me to."

"And I am requesting that you go come. John and I will manage. Mary's here. You have work today, don't you?"

He sighed and then nodded. "I do. Call me if you need me? I just know Abe won't be happy."

"That's his problem, not yours. You stayed and now you're going home. We'll be fine."

She watched as he walked away and then followed to lock the door after him. She knew she should have let him stay but something was telling her to make him leave. She turned to stare at the bedroom. Somehow she had to get John and Mary to leave and that wouldn't happen easily. She leant back against the door, fatigue weighing her down. She knew Abe would be there but she really wasn't in the mood to talk to anyone else tonight. She found her phone, sent Abe a message not to come, to come later that morning. All was quiet, she reported.

Abe stared at the house, not willing to return home. Joseph had found a credible threat, which had been confirmed, that someone was after Larkin now, not just Tierney. They were frantically working to confirm who. He had spoken to both Frankie and Caleb, waking them up to do so. Caleb had requested that Abe or one of his men stay with Larkin and Tierney until they could sort out what was happening. Matt had paused beside his truck, shaking his head.

Abe had stared at him when he reported that Larkin had told him to go home, that he needed to work that day, and that he needed to be with Sarah.

Abe had watched Matt drive away before he reached for his phone and found Larkin's message. *That's not happening, Larkin. Even if you don't let me in, I am not leaving here.* He turned his head as he saw headlights approached and then was out of his truck, walking towards Frankie.

"Frankie?"

"You were right, Abe. We've confirmed it. Eddie said he and Ben would be over this morning and wouldn't leave, not matter what she said." Eddie Brown and Ben Johnson were retired police officers who had responded to Frankie's request.

"Good. Eddie's about as stubborn as you can get."

"Reminds me of someone else." Frankie grinned at Abe's smile, knowing Eddie was an uncle to Abe. He nodded towards the house. "Matt still there?"

"Nope. She sent him home. It's just John and Mary and I know John has to be at Emergency for his shift by four."

Frankie shook his head. "That's not good." He stalked towards the house, anger simmering just below the surface and knocked at the door, finally calling for Larkin to open up, that he needed to talk to her.

Larkin sighed from where she was still leaning against the door. John had left through the back door and headed for where he had parked his car, stating he would be back, to call if she needed him. Mary had had to leave with him. She didn't like the feeling of danger she felt but she had no thoughts of anything but Tierney and what she needed to do for him.

She finally turned, opening the door, letting both Frankie and Abe inside. She stared at the two, not sure what they were doing there at that time of the morning, but she could feel fear starting to rise within her. She turned and paced for the kitchen, reaching to start the coffee she knew they would want, before she turned, pointing to the chairs.

"I need to check on Tierney. Help yourselves to the coffee when it's ready. I'll be back as soon as I can." She was out of the kitchen before they could stop her.

Abe stared at her and then at Frankie, before he grinned at the look on Frankie's face.

"She's independent, Frankie. She had too much restriction in her life. Her family didn't realize how they had treated her. She's just getting independence, found herself married to someone she didn't know well, and has been abducted and her husband hurt. How is she to fee?"

Frankie nodded. "I agree with you, Abe. She'll break soon under this if we don't solve it."

Abe shook his head. "She won't break. She'll bend but not break." He turned his head as he heard her footsteps.

Larkin poured herself a cup of coffee, her eyes heavy, almost asleep on her feet, before she turned and pulled out a chair, seating herself, setting the mug on the table and wrapping her hands around it, her eyes on Abe and Frankie.

"Why are you two here? I did send Matt home, Abe."

"I know you did. I talked to him. I was here as he left." Abe's face grew stern. "What part of you're in danger and a target don't you get?"

She jumped at the harsh tone before she glared at him. "Don't start with me, Abe. You keep saying this but haven't shown me any proof. Tierney told me I'm not the one they wanted. They told him that."

"He said that?" Frankie looked over at Abe before watching her.

"He did. Matt and John both heard him." She struggled with her emotions. "Why did they do that to him, Abe?"

"I don't know, Larkin. It has to be something with that manuscript. Emma has Jace working on what she found."

"That's good, but I doubt it will solve this." She sighed, her head going back as she looked up, a prayer in her heart for protection and healing for Tierney. *Lord, heal, protect him. I don't care what happens to me as long as he survives.*

Frankie had been watching her closely, then reached for the file he had set in front of him. "Larkin, these are photos that we have found. Take a look at them, please? Tell me if you recognize anyone."

She reached for the folder, her hand resting on it for a moment, knowing that everything would be changed once she opened it up. She prayed, her eyes rising to study the doorway to the hall, wanting to run to Tierney but knowing he was sleeping, but that he would back any decision she made. That much she had learned about him.

She slowly opened the file, staring at the first picture, and then leafing through them, a frown establishing itself on her brow. She flipped back to the beginning, sorting them, pausing at a couple, before she looked up at Frankie.

"What are you actually asking me with these, Frankie?"

"I just need to know if you are familiar with any of them."

He waited as she looked back through them, finally sliding four over towards him.

"These ones. I know these one. God help me, I didn't know. I didn't know they would be trouble. I only met them once or twice at the most, through work." Tears sparkled on her cheeks before she was on her feet, running from the room. She stood for a moment, her face turned towards the kitchen, before she crossed the room to drop to a sitting position beside Tierney, her arms wrapping around him and her face against his shoulders as sobs shook her.

Did I do this, Lord? Did I bring trouble to him? But I didn't know him before. I had no idea who he was when we went in. Maybe the boys did but they said no. Lord, please? We need answers and don't seem to be able to find any.

## Chapter 32

Abe paced the living room, his eyes occasionally turning towards the hall and then towards the kitchen where Frankie was on a conference call. Things were going wrong, he thought, and I have no idea how to fix them. He turned as he heard Frankie's footsteps coming towards him.

"Abe, we verified the photos she picked out. She was right. She knew them through work. I've sent out detectives and patrol officers to bring them in for questioning. I can't guarantee we'll find them all though."

"That's what I'm afraid of. That you won't find them and they'll come after her."

"Who will come after me?" Larkin spoke from the doorway.

Abe spun, not having heard her. "How is Tierney?"

"He's still sleeping, for now. He hasn't roused since Matt was here. Thank God for that." She glanced between the two men. "Who is after me?"

Frankie pointed to a chair. "Sit, please, Larkin?"

She stared at him, a mutinous look on her face, before she walked to the couch and sat, her eyes on him.

"You shouldn't have let Matt leave, Larkin. We have word the ones after you are right here in your neighbourhood. Right now." Frankie was stern with her, knowing he had to be.

"I don't really care, Frankie. He needed to go home. John and Mary had to leave. What was I do to?"

"Why were you so insistent Matt leave, Larkin?" Abe's quiet question brought her attention to where he was sitting beside her.

She shrugged. "I don't know, Abe, to tell you the truth. I just knew he had to. And I don't like it that you two are here. That puts you in danger as well."

Abe gave a half-smile. "Larkin, it's what we do, who we are. We protect people. Frankie here is a police officer and you know what they do."

She nodded, her eyes thoughtful. "I know, but there is just something that's not right about the whole thing." She turned as she heard a sound from Tierney and was on her feet, dropping to a kneeling position beside him.

"Larkin? You're okay?" Tierney didn't realize he was repeating himself.

"I am. And you?"

He shook his head. "I don't know, Larkin. Can I sit up?"

She helped him up, stuffing pillows behind him to lean back on. She frowned even as she helped him hold a glass of juice to drink from.

Tierney stared at the doorway. "Who's here, Larkin?"

"Abe is. So is Frankie."

"They are. Good. I need to talk to Frankie." He shoved at the covers. "I need to be on my feet, Larkin. We're in danger."

"Tierney, you're not strong enough yet."

Tierney shook his head. "I need up. Please, Larkin, just help. If you won't, I either do it myself or I yell for Abe or Frankie."

She finally reached to help him, her arms around him as he walked towards the living room, somewhat more stable on his feet. She watched as Frankie and Abe walked towards them, hands out to help. Tierney settled on the couch, Larkin beside him, before he wrapped an arm around her and pulled her tight to him.

"Abe, thank you. I know what it was like where I was. I can never repay you. Frankie, you're here. Can you take my statement? I only want to go over it once."

"We can do that, Tierney. Just let me grab my briefcase." Frankie was on his feet and out the door before Tierney could respond.

Frankie settled back down, his dictator ready, his notebook and pen in hand, as he watched Tierney carefully, knowing he would tell his story whether or not he was able to. He exchanged a look with Abe who shrugged and then rose to head for the kitchen, returning with a tray of mugs of coffee and a mug of broth for Tierney.

"Tierney, I'll let you talk. Then if I have any questions, I ask them at the end. Larkin, you'll have to let him talk. I know you want him to wait but time is of the essence here now, given the threats against both of you."

Tierney nodded, his eyes on Larkin, knowing she was hurting for him just as he was hurting for her. Whoever was responsible had taken a lot from them both, time they would never get back, and he regretted that. God alone knew when this would be over. He prayed soon.

## Chapter 33

Tierney's arm tightened around Larkin, seeking to comfort her just as she did him. He watched her upturned face, seeing the emotions flickering through her eyes, emotions she would not let the other two men see. He sighed, not wanting her to hear what had happened, but knowing that she would. She would not be his Larkin if she didn't want to know.

He laid his head back for a moment, gathering his strength, sorting through his thoughts, emotions, and memories. He knew this would be a very difficult time for him, just trying to say what he needed to, but for himself, it was something he needed to do.

Tierney finally began to speak, his voice low at times, at times tight with fear and anger. Larkin's hands found his and held on tight, not complaining when his would tighten on hers.

Tierney went back to the night they were taken, remembering how they had been sitting on the back deck. He didn't state their words, his eyes on Larkin, who nodded. Those were words for between them and them only. He remembered the feeling of fear as a weapon was held to his neck and they were forced to their feet, Larkin moved away from him and then forced in a van.

He tried hard to see anything about the van but didn't have time, the hand on his back propelling into the van where he landed on his hands and knees, spinning to watch the door pulled down and the lock clicked into place.

He crawled forward even as the van moved away from their home, searching in the blackness for Larkin, wrapping his arms around her when he found her, finding a corner he could wedge them into, taking the brunt of the van's movement, his heart raised in frantic prayer for safety and release.

He felt the van finally turn a corner and then move along a rough road at a slower speed. He frowned in the dark, his mind raising as to where they were. He had no idea. He heard the whimper of fear from Larkin as the door was raised and a bright light was shone at them, their arms raising to block it. Coarse voices ordered them out of the van. He jumped down, carrying Larkin, finding himself shoved away from her and hearing Larkin fighting with the men before he heard her body hit the ground. He spun, fighting to get back to her, his arms twisting violently behind his back as he was shoved forward towards a building and then through doors into a cell. He hit the wall on the side opposite the door.

He thrust himself from the wall, hitting the door as it closed and locked. His fists pounded at it and he shook the knob, pushing at the door itself to get out. His shouts rang through the room. His calls for Larkin went unanswered. He listened but did not hear her at all. He pressed his ear to the door, not hearing her, and that both worried and scared him. He had no idea where she was.

He turned to look at the room, his eyes searching in the dim light. He spun as he heard the door opening, raising an arm once more to block the light shone at him. He heard one of the men walking towards him and once more the clanking of shackles. He backed away until he had no room to back away. He fought the men as they tried to shackle his legs, finally taken to the ground and held face down as the shackles were fastened. He lay there after they left and the door looked behind them once more. He shuddered in sudden fright. Was this was Larkin faced, shackles as well? Lord, protect my lady, my love. Don't let them hurt her.

He finally rose, searching the room over and over, trying to find a way out. The windows were too small, he could not squeeze through them. There was nothing he could use as a weapon to defend himself or fight his way out with. He slumped down on the pallet they had provided him, his legs stretched out in front of him, his head back against the wall. His eyes slid closed as he prayed, praying as he had never before in his life. He needed to get out. He needed to find Larkin and bring her to safety. That was his plan and his goal.

He had dozed off when the door flew open and he was yanked to his feet, propelled through the door before he was completely awake and to another room, where he has pulled to a stop, a weapon shoved into his lower back. He blinked against the light, seeing it was early morning. He heard a whimper and tried to turn but the weapon dug in even harder. His heart broke as he watched Larkin shoved roughly towards a chair and then down into it. Her hair flowed forward to cover her face as the man behind her held his hand on her neck, forcing her to look down.

Tierney struggled to reach her, not caring about the weapon in his back until a brutal blow dropped him to his knees. He gasped for breath, his arms wrapping around his abdomen. He finally stood before he was slammed into a chair, his eyes on Larkin, who could not look at him for how she was held. His eyes turned to the man behind the light.

"What do you want? Let her go."

"Not happening. You have something we want. She stays here until you give it to us."

"I don't know what it is you want. There is nothing in that manuscript that would be of benefit to you."

"That's where you're wrong. There is something in there. And I think you have found it. Turn it over to us and you go free."

"I don't have it. Let her go." Tierney struggled to escape the hands now holding him, but was unable to. He felt himself dragged away from Larkin, struggling to get to her, struggling to walk, his feet tangling in the chain between them.

Shoved abruptly into the room, he hit his hands and knees as he heard the door slam shut. His head hung down. Larkin was alive, that's all that mattered. He shifted so he could sit on the floor, his eyes on the door, his heart sinking at being a captive again.

He was pulled from his room every day after that, usually in the early morning. He slept in fits and starts. He didn't get a good look at Larkin to see how she was, but he could tell she had lost weight. Please, Lord, get us out of here.

Then one day, he was pulled from the room and stood for a number of hours before the leader appeared.

"Where's Larkin?"

The leader gave a cruel laugh. "She's not coming back."

"Where is she? What did you do to her?"

The leader laughed harder. "She's not coming back. She's dead."

"No, she's not. Where is she?"

The leader walked towards him, shadowed by the light behind him. "I told you. She's dead. We got rid of her body. So, you see, it's just you now." A blow across Tierney's face snapped his head to the side. "If you had cooperated, then she would still be alive."

Tierney broke free from the men holding him and leapt at the leader, taking him to the floor, his hands shoving at the man's shoulder. "Where is she? She is not dead."

Pulled from the leader and dragged back to his cell, Tierney's body twisted and turned as he tried to escape. He had to get away. He had to find her.

Despair grew within him as day after day went by. He refused to answer when he was spoken to. He didn't eat, couldn't eat, and only drank enough water to quench what little thirst he had. He grew weak, shaking as he was forced to stand for hours. He sought sleep but was awakened every few hours. He knew what they were up to. Psychological torture, he decided. He had come to the point he couldn't even pray, but he knew God heard his silent, anxious prayers. He despaired that he would see Larkin again. He would likely die in captivity.

He retreated in his mind, not thinking, not trying to figure out anything. He finally just slept, not even rousing when the men came for him that last day. They stood watching him before they walked away, back to their leader. Their leader was not happy, that much they knew. He wanted information from Tierney who wouldn't or couldn't provide it for him.

## Chapter 34

Tierney didn't hear the quiet steps moving his way or the click of the door unlocking. He didn't feel the hands that reached for him and pulled him to his feet. He roused at that point, protesting that he didn't have what they wanted. They had the wrong man. And no, Larkin couldn't be dead. He would know it if she was.

He was shoved gently into a vehicle with a man on either side of him. He slumped in the seat, finally raising his eyes, to realize that the shackles had been taken from his legs. He looked at the man on his right.

"Abe?"

"That's right, Tierney. You're safe. We have you now."

"Thank you, Lord." Tierney subsided into silence, not wanting to ask but needing to. "Larkin?"

"She's at home, Tierney. Micah and Kat are with her."

"She's alive?" Hope sprang into Tierney's face.

"She is. Why?" Abe shared a look with Ian on Tierney's other side.

"They told me she was dead. They told me that every day. I gave up." He slumped back once more, his face contorting even as tears dropped from his eyes, tears he couldn't stop and didn't care that they came.

Abe's hand rested on his shoulder. "She's alive. We found out where they had left her and went in and got her. She hasn't given up hope that you'll come home. She's grieving you, though."

Tierney nodded. "I suspected she would be." He drew a deep breath. "We had just told each other of our love for one another when we were taken."

The four men in the vehicle exchanged glances, horrified at the timing and at the treatment they had undergone. They knew Tierney would need help.

"Do you know who it was?" Ian's question brought Tierney's head up.

Tierney shook his head, which was almost too much of an effort for him. "No, but his voice sounded familiar. I couldn't see him, he always stood in front of a light. Even when I tackled him, I couldn't make out who it was."

"You tackled him and lived?" Ian's voice showed his surprise.

"I did. That was when he told me Larkin was dead." Tierney grew quiet, his strength gone, fatigue weighing him down. "Where was I?"

"At a building just inside the city limits. They drove around likely for a while, from what Larkin has said."

Tierney nodded. "Where did you find her?"

"In the caves on the other side of town. It was strange. The ETD went in, found her, brought her out, and then the caves were destroyed in an explosion."

"An explosion? After you got out? That is bizarre." Tierney watched as Joseph, who was driving, pulled into his driveway. "I'm home. Is Larkin here?"

Abe threw a puzzled look at Matt in the front seat. "She is, Tierney. She's waiting for you."

Tierney nodded. "Good. Can I go home now?"

Abe smiled. "You are home, Tierney. We'll get you to Larkin as soon as you're out of the vehicle. Just take your time."

Abe stood for a moment, watching Tierney before he looked up at the house, seeing Larkin in the front door. He nodded even as he gave her a smile and he saw the relief in her face.

Tierney shifted slowly so his legs were outside of the vehicle, Abe helping him to stand on shaking legs, Matt reaching to help. Arms around them, he made his way to the stairs, pausing, knowing he had to climb them and not sure if he had enough strength to do that. Slowly he made his way up them, stopping at the top to gather his strength and then inching for the door, searching for Larkin. He saw her and then they were in each other's arms, sobs shaking both their bodies.

Guided to the suite on the main floor, showered and in clean clothes, he crept into the bed, knowing Larkin was in the same house, even if not in the same room. He slept, knowing he was safe at home, but not yet safe. He also knew nightmares would once more plague him. He wanted Larkin not to know, but he needed the comfort she and only she could bring.

He awoke in the night to find Larkin kneeling beside him, her arm around him, her hand over his heart. She had brought comfort to him that only she could. He could rest now.

Tierney paused, looking at Frankie, who nodded.

"I have your statement, Tierney. I'll have it transcribed and then have you read it over and sign it." He shared a look with Abe. "You have no idea who it was?"

Tierney shook his head in an exhausted manner, his eyes on his empty mug. "No. I should though. I have met him somewhere or talked to him at some point. Do you know who he is?"

Frankie shared another look with Abe. "We have an idea, but we need to do some more investigations before we're sure. We need to keep you two safe. He'll be looking here for you."

"I know he will. Abe, can you take that manuscript and get rid of it?"

"Let Frankie take it into evidence. He'll need it after all. It seems to be the whole reason for what you two have faced."

"He can have it." Tierney made a move to stand, stopping as Larkin tightened her hold on him.

"Frankie can get it, Tierney. He'll need to put it into a bag, anyway."

Frankie was on his feet. "It's on your desk, Tierney?"

"It was. I have no idea where it is now."

"It's where Emma and I left it yesterday, Frankie. You know where." Larkin watched him walk away before she frowned at Abe, who was shaking his head at her. "Abe?"

"Frankie's right, you know. We need to move you two."

"But you can't. You have people in for training this week."

"But we have a secret weapon. My uncle and a friend. Both are retired officers who are stopping in this morning, on the pretext of visiting you. They will move you somewhere safe."

"And just where would that be?"

Abe shook his head again. "We're not saying, Larkin. We can't be sure someone isn't listening in."

She stared at him for a moment, her eyes growing huge as she caught what he meant. "Then, I guess I should pack for us." She turned her head to study Tierney, finding him sleeping. "Abe, can we lay him down? He'll be more comfortable."

"That we can do. I'll do that while you go pack."

"But what do I pack? How do I know what to pack when I don't know where we're going."

"Casual stuff. Jeans, sweatshirts, sweaters, T-shirts, shorts, personal stuff. You get the drift, I think, Larkin."

"I do. I just don't like it." She sounded grumpy, she knew, but just didn't care. She ran up the stairs, heading for her own bedroom, and then she stopped inside the door, a groan coming from her. Lord, that wasn't nice or polite. He's trying to keep us safe, only I don't know that they can. I am trying to trust, to find that strong tower, to hide under Your wings, and praying that Tierney is too, but it's so hard.

She quickly packed a duffle bag for herself and then headed for Tierney's room, hesitating inside the door. She really didn't know what he had. She had avoided the room since they were married, not sure how he felt about her. Even now, even when he had told her he loved her, there was doubt and hesitation. I love him so much, Lord, but what if he no longer loves me like he said? What do I do? She waited, not willing to move, until she felt a peace sweep over her. She knew then she didn't have to worry about that. Not right now. Right now, she had to pack for Tierney and go with the two men Abe said would be there.

## *Chapter 35*

Larkin moved around the apartment they had been taken to by Eddie and Ben, hidden in the back of a van that Eddie had pulled into their garage. He assured her that he and Ben had done this before. In fact, Ben's son and niece had had adventures as had Abe's sister, Rebecca. She had shaken her head at them, not quite sure if they were in fact telling the truth.

She had promised to stay in the apartment but was getting nervous about being in one place. She turned as she heard Tierney's footsteps approaching her before he swept her into a hug. He was getting stronger each day but she knew he was not sleeping at night. She had lost track of the times she had flown to him in the night, calming him with her touch and being calmed by his. She needed his comfort at this time but she was afraid for him.

Frankie had asked if they had received any packages, letters, threats, phone calls or text messages and she had shook her head and remarked that they should have. Frankie had agreed, stating that puzzled him. He had searched their phones and she had even checked her email and the work email and found nothing. She had stood and stared at him as he had paced the apartment.

Tierney stood for a moment before he guided Larkin to the couch, sitting and then drawing her close to him, fatigue washing over him for a moment.

"Tierney? Are you okay?"

He shrugged, his eyes on her. "I really don't know, Larkin. I'm exhausted, worn out, and discouraged."

"You are entitled to be that. With what you've been through all these months, I can't imagine you feeling any other way."

"I know, my love. I was so praying and hoping this would be over by now. I want to get on with life."

She grew silent, her eyes on her hands, not wanting to look at him and see that he wanted to set her free.

"Larkin?" He waited but she didn't raise her head. "Larkin, please, my love? Look at me." When she finally did, he reached to touch her face. "I meant what I said. I love you deeply, more and more each day. I just want this over so we can get on with our life together."

"Me, too." Her voice was barely audible. "I love you too, Tierney. It almost killed me when he said you were dead and then they dumped me in that cave. I don't remember it at all. I think they drugged me or something. I know I was awake and then the next thing, I'm safe."

He rested his chin on her head. "Both of us have been through so much. We need to be safe again and we can't. I just wish I knew who it was."

"It will come. Frankie showed me a bunch of photos that last night we were at home. I recognized some but I'm not sure from where. Work, I think." She looked up at him. "Speaking of work, where are you on your manuscripts?"

He sighed. "I have two or three that are outstanding. I talked to the clients and told them what had happened. They want to wait. Said I was the best at what I do." He paused, a though coming to him. "I need to ask Eddie or Ben if they could bring them to me. And a laptop that I can secure tightly."

"That would work for you. But what about me?"

"What about you?"

"What am I do to?"

He hugged her. "I'll teach you what I do. Then we'll have two eyes to work on them. In fact, you can take courses on line for that." He searched her face, his hand coming up to touch her cheek. "you are so beautiful." He reached to kiss her, surprising her at first. When he leaned back, he studied her face. "I pray we live for a long time."

She gave him a smile but he could see the worry in her eyes. "I do too, Tierney. But I am so afraid."

"I am, for you. Not for me." Tierney sighed as he heard a tap at the door. "We just don't seem to get a chance to talk." He rose, heading for the door, listening for the words that he needed to hear before he opened it to find Frankie and Caleb standing there. He stepped back to let them it, suddenly knowing something had broken in the case, but not sure he wanted to hear.

Larkin had shifted on the couch, waiting to see who had entered. She shook her head. "I don't like it when you come around, Frankie. You never have any good news."

Frankie laughed at her even as he sat, sliding a file folder onto the coffee table. "I'm sorry you think that, Larkin. And just how are you feeling?"

She glared at him for a moment. "You know how I feel. Caged. Forgotten. Empty. Wanting my home. Wanting my life back." She sighed as both Caleb and Frankie grinned at her. "Did I get my point across? And how soon?"

"Soon, Larkin. Soon." Caleb looked with compassion as her. "We have found the four that you pointed out. They are under arrest at this moment and will be questioned as soon as we can. You did good."

"I may have done good but not good enough." She snuggled closer to Tierney, needing the comfort and calming he brought her. "How soon?"

"Soon, I promise." Caleb looked at Tierney. "That manuscript, Tierney? The techs have been going over it with a fine tooth comb, as they say. They tell me you had made a huge start in solving the mystery, doing most of their work for them. And then Larkin finding the numbers and letters on the edging? That has propelled the investigation ahead."

Frankie took up the conversation. "The people we arrested? You were right when you said you knew them from work. They had been there, apparently for an appointment but they did say it was to find out about you. You were a target at that point, but they decided not to go ahead with anything to do with you at that point. They took Tierney captive to try and have him work on the manuscript when he was captive but they couldn't find it. They tried breaking into his home and searching but it wasn't there."

Tierney gave a small laugh. "The thing of it is that it was. I have locked boxes that I put the manuscripts in when I'm not working on them. They fit into a room behind a bookshelf."

Larkin nodded. "That they do. No one would know the room was there. It's certainly not evident. Tierney only has the one out that he's working on and that gets locked into a safe at night." She turned to look at him. "We didn't do that with this one. Why not?"

"I don't think we had time. And then again, I didn't think it was that old or important." Tierney shared a look with Caleb. "Apparently it was more important than I thought."

"It was, Tierney. The techs are running with what you did and what Emma has provided. The detectives have tracked some of the accounts to banks overseas. We have search warrants in the works to seize them. They are clearly the gains from crime."

Larkin frowned. "Crime? What kind?"

"Thefts and sales of antiquities apparently. That's why the manuscript is so important to them." Caleb looked over at Frankie.

Frankie continued the line of thought. "We have identified the men who kidnapped you the first time, Tierney. They are what we call thugs for hire. They set up the jail you were found in. The other people you heard? Homeless people they kidnapped and used against you, to make you think you really were in a jail."

"They did? I thought I was in a real jail outside the country. I don't remember much that day I was taken. I think they drugged me or something so I didn't know where I was. I just remember waking up in that cell with the shackles on." He frowned, his eyes on Larkin. "I don't get that. Why shackle us? What was the point?"

"To make sure you didn't run. To wear you down psychologically. To prove they were in control. There are a number of different reasons they would do this." Frankie leaned back, studying the folder he had set down, knowing he had to show the contents and really not wanting to.

"Frankie." When he looked at her, Larkin pointed to the folder he had been contemplating. "What's in there?"

## Chapter 36

Frankie pulled the folder towards him, opening and closing it before he looked first at Tierney and then at Larkin. "What is in the folder is what we have so far, what we can share, that is. We were not prepared for what we found." Frankie handed Tierney the folder, with a word of caution. "I don't think you're prepared for this, Tierney. I wasn't."

Tierney looked at him and then down at the folder before looking at Larkin. "It's that bad?"

"We think it is." Caleb finally spoke, compassion in his voice. "This will take you back to when you born, Tierney, and to your parents." He shared a look with Frankie, before looking at Larkin. "And somehow, Larkin, that has involved you. We have an idea we're investigating but we can't say for sure yet what."

She sighed, her head going down on Tierney's shoulder for a moment. "That's about what I thought you'd say. You are making this so difficult, you know? Why couldn't we have the normal everyday adventure like everyone else?"

Her plaintive question caused the three men to laugh, and she smirked at them, getting the response she had wanted. Caleb shook his finger at her, then pointed at Tierney.

"Tierney, we need you to go through that. If you want to leave it for now and we can walk away, that's fine. We just need it done today."

Tierney looked down at Larkin and then at the folder. "Caleb, please. Pray first. We need that."

"Gladly, my friend." Caleb prayed, his petition bringing tears to Larkin's eyes which she swiped at angrily.

Tierney's hand rested on the folder as he studied it before he opened it, staring at the top photo. "My parents?"

"That's correct, Tierney. Somehow we found discovered they obtained the account numbers and used them. We are still investigating how."

Tierney turned to the next photo, Larkin's hand on his as she studied it. "That's you, Tierney, at what age?"

"I think four, maybe. That's when I first began to ask about my parents. No one could explain where they were or else they wouldn't. I didn't know until I was in my late teens what actually happened. I found that out by searching newspaper archives." He looked up, bleakness on his face. "Do you know how hard it is to grow up with that stigma?"

He looked at the next photo and then the next, moving through them, hesitating at some, almost speaking and then keeping quiet. He paused at the last one, a frown in place, before he looked at Larkin.

"Larkin?"

She was studying the photo before she looked up at him. "That's at the college basketball game. I was there with the boys. Lincoln and Logan were supposed to be there but they weren't. And you are sitting right beside Peter! That's strange. I don't remember that."

"I do. I remember sitting with Peter and talking to James. But I don't remember you. I should if you were there."

"The boys were sitting side by side. I was late getting there and they saved a seat for me. I was on the opposite side from you." She reached for the picture. "This was taken in the last half, that I can remember. But who's that behind you? She's not watching the game. She's watching you."

"She is." He looked up at the other two men. "Did you notice that?"

Caleb and Frankie shared a look before Frankie reached for the photo. "No, I don't think we did. The woman behind you? Is that the one, Larkin?"

"It is."

"She resembles you, did you notice?" Caleb tilted his head to study the photo. "Is she our missing link? And how do we find her?"

"Emma. Talk to Emma." Frankie pulled out his phone, took a close up of the woman and sent it on to Emma. He watched as a quick response came back. "Emma's good. She already has a name and a stock of information on this woman, she says."

"Good. That will help." Caleb finally stood. "Keep those and let us know if anything else comes to you. We'll find them, Tierney. We'll get you back your life. It's taken too much time already."

Tierney stood and walked to the door, pausing before he opened it for them. "I think this is it, that whoever it is will come after me again. But how do they find me if I'm hiding?"

"We're not ready to put you out there yet, Tierney. At some point, we may."

He sighed. "I know, but Larkin can't take much of this. She's getting ready to run. And if she runs, I'm with her."

Frankie shook his head. "They always do. Just don't let her talk to Ian. He'll offer to fly her somewhere we can't find her."

Tierney stared at him even as Larkin wrapped an arm around him. "He does that?"

Larkin laughed, having heard that before. "Apparently he has offered to fly just about every lady in trouble somewhere they can hide." She reached for her phone, frowning at it and then beginning to laugh. "And guess who just sent a text!"

"Ian. Where does he want to fly you two to?" Frankie shook his head as he said good bye.

Tierney paced the apartment late that night. He was exhausted but knew if he slept the dreams would come. He had awakened Larkin the night before with them and she told him she had despaired of calming him.

Larkin watched him before looking back at the photos. "Tierney, come. Sit for a moment."

He sat beside her, an arm around her as she leaned back against him. "What is it, my love?"

"Didn't you say your parents died from a drug overdose? Did you ever request autopsy reports on them?"

He shook his head. "I didn't. I guess I should have. Maybe Frankie can for us."

She nodded, before pointing to a picture, showing him as an adult. "When would this have been taken?"

He studied it. "About seven months or so ago. Why?"

"Look closely at it. That man watching you. He looks like you will in about thirty years."

Tierney frowned at her before he took the photo, tilting it to see it better. "You're right. This is bizarre." He reached for his phone, dialing Frankie's number. "Frankie? Larkin discovered something. The photo you numbered at 24. There's a man watching us. She says it looks a lot like me."

Frankie paused, sorting through the pictures on his home office desk. "Which man?"

"The one off to the right, in the red plaid shirt."

"Him?" Frankie groaned. "We missed that, you know. Does Larkin want a job?"

Tierney laughed as he turned to her. "I doubt it very much."

## Chapter 37

The next morning found Larkin dressed and pulling on her sneakers as Tierney emerged from the kitchen. He frowned at her. What is she up to, Lord? Why do I feel like we're going on the offensive?

"Larkin?"

Tierney's question stopped her hands as she was tying her shoelace before she finished and looked up at him. "I'm tired of this, Tierney. I am tired of you not having a life. I am tired of running, of being restricted. We need the freedom to move on. I have searched for that strong tower God has promised us but not found it. Have you?"

He sank to the floor beside her, his arm around her. "This has been hard on you, Larkin. I'm sorry. I'm sorry you had to get involved and went through what you did. I'm just not sorry you're here with me. God has protected us. He has provided that strong tower." He watched her face. "Where are you heading, my love?"

She shrugged. "I need out of here, Tierney. I can't handle being caged. Not after that prison."

He nodded. "I know, my love." He reached for his own shoes, pulling them on, then rising and holding out a hand for her. "Can I interest you in a walk?"

"Most certainly. I just don't know that Caleb and Frankie will say." She paused as a tap came to the door. "We weren't expecting anyone, were we?"

Tierney shook his head. "Not that I was aware of." He peeked through the peep hole. "You were talking about Frankie, and here he is. But something is off with him."

"We should let him in."

Tierney shook his head. "No, I'm not sure that it's him." He reached for his phone and dialed. "Frankie?"

"Tierney? What's up? Did Larkin recognize someone else?" Frankie sounded normal, causing Tierney to turn and stare at the door.

"Frankie, where are you?"

"At home. Why?"

"Because someone who looks almost like you is at our door. Right now."

"Tierney, into the kitchen. There's another entrance I don't know if you were told about. It's hidden. Are you there? Okay, see the pantry?"

"Yeah. What about it?"

"Feel along the side of it. You should find a catch."

"Found it. Well! What do you know? A hidden staircase." He gripped Larkin's hand, pulling her into it and then swinging the door closed behind them. "Where does it lead, Frankie?"

"To the stock room of the store below you. Head down and then out the back door. Be careful. They may be watching." Frankie sounded out of breath and Tierney knew he was running for his vehicle. "I'll be there in ten. I'll have officers there in two."

"Thanks, Frankie." He pulled Larkin down the stairs, shoving open the panel at the foot and then shoving it closed behind them. He headed for the back door, cracking it carefully open before leaving the store, Larkin's hand tight in his, and walking quickly away.

"Where are we heading?" Larkin peeked behind her.

"Away from here. I would like to know how they found us. Eddie assured me no one knew about this place." He stopped. "Your phone?"

"My phone? I left it in the apartment. What about yours?"

Tierney leaned casually against a building, his focus on his phone as he searched it. "And here we go. There's an app installed that has been tracking us." He turned off his phone and stared down at it.

"Do you have to get rid of it?"

"I hope not to. It has information on it that I use." He raised his eyes to stare at her, an unreadable look in his eyes. "I'm sorry, Larkin. I didn't know."

"I know that. You would have dealt with it." She looked around. "We can't leave it anywhere. That puts others at risk." She grabbed it and ran for a building, back in a few minutes.

"Where did you leave?"

She began to laugh. "I handed it to the police officer at the front desk and asked that she give it to Frankie or Caleb and why. She tried to get me to stay." She looked around. "Now, let's blow this joint as they say."

Tierney swept her into a hug, laughing at her nonsense. "You do my heart so much good, my love."

"I do?" She looked up at him. "And you mine. Now where?"

Tierney looked around and then walked rapidly away from the apartment. "Frankie will find us. At least I hope he will. There. That's his car, isn't it?"

"I'm not sure, but there is certainly a lot of activity around that building. He didn't waste any time, did he?"

"No, he didn't. They don't, from what I understand." Tierney stopped at a vendor, buying them a coffee each, and then pointing to a bench. "Let's wait there. Frankie will find us. I asked the vendor to let him know where we were."

"Was that safe?" Larkin sipped at her coffee, enjoying the flavour.

"I pray it was. We had to let them know we're safe." He looked around, feeling eyes on him. "We're being watched, Larkin. We didn't throw them off, after all."

She leaned her head against him, seeking comfort. "I didn't think we had. I just wonder how many groups there are?"

"What do you mean? You think there is more than one?"

"I would suspect there is. Isn't there always at least two or three groups?"

Tierney grinned again, his eyes on the man approaching them. "Here's Ben."

Ben slid down beside Larkin, his eyes studying the two before he looked away. "Frankie called. Said you had a visitor."

"We did. I almost opened the door but something just wasn't him."

"It's a good thing you didn't. Frankie got word to me. That was a hired assassin."

Larkin's breath drew in sharply and her hand tightened in Tierney's grasp.

Tierney watched her even as he spoke. "Hired assassin? Which one of us?"

"That we have to determine. Here comes Frankie. He wants to separate you two and then get you to the department. I agree with him. I'll take you with me, Tierney. Larkin, Frankie will have you with him."

Larkin rose as Frankie approached, walking towards him, hearing Ben and Tierney walk the opposite direction. She paused as she neared Frankie, not quite sure if it was him, given what had happened.

"It really is me, Larkin." He grinned as she drew a deep breath. "I know. We have the man in custody as well as three others who were waiting for him. They seem to be upping the ante right now, trying to get to you two."

"And did your techs solve the mystery?"

"They have." Frankie shot a quick look around. "In here." He shoved her towards a store and then through it and out a back door.

"Frankie, I'm getting tired of running through stores and out their back door. Someone's going to complain about me doing that soon."

Frankie shook his head, his eyes searching. "In there, Larkin. Get down into as small a crouch as you can get. Don't come out except for me or Caleb." He shoved her towards a sheltered spot, walking away from her.

She did what he asked, her arms covering her face as she heard him talking to someone and then the sound of a weapon discharging. She jumped, her face raised for a moment, before she hid it again. She heard footsteps approaching and didn't move, knowing Frankie would call her by name. She didn't see the man when he spotted her and then grinned. He had her, he thought.

She jumped as she felt a hand touch her hair, twisting it and yanking her to her feet. She reached to try and get away, but couldn't. She was pulled from her hiding spot and towards where Frankie lay on the ground, his hands cuffed behind him. Forced to her knees, the man's hand still twisting her hair, she prayed as she had not prayed before. This is it, isn't it, Lord? I'm not walking away. Please let Frankie live. I couldn't bear it if he died because of me. Let Tierney know how much I do love him. And Lord, when it happens today, let me go quickly? That's all I ask.

## Chapter 38

Caleb's head raised and then he was on his feet, heading towards Doug as he heard him calling for him.

"Doug?"

"It's Frankie. His beacon went off." Doug was running for the back door, his team ahead of him.

Caleb ran after him, heading for his vehicle, popping the trunk to grab his body armour and then heading for the ETF van.

"Where?"

"Downtown somewhere. It just went off." Doug knew it wasn't an accident that Frankie's beacon went off. All the officers were equipped with a sensor that if they went down and stayed down for a certain period of time without moving it sounded an alarm in the department.

Caleb watched closely as the ETF members suited up quickly, ready to head out as soon as they stopped. The van slowed and then halted, Doug looking through the windshield.

"I see him, Caleb. Larkin's with him. But who is that who has her?"

Caleb spun to stare as well. "This isn't good. He's the other assassin our people are looking for. How did he find her? Tierney's safe with Ben in a conference room."

The men exited quietly, heading in a circle around the three in the centre of the back alley. Doug could heard whimpers from Larkin as he closed in, his eyes on the man holding her, and then flickering to Frankie, who laid still. Please, Lord, was his prayer, let him be okay. I don't want to be the one to explain to Darcy, nor does Caleb.

Larkin twisted and turned, trying to escape, her voice quiet but tortured as she questioned the man, her eyes on Frankie's still body.

"Why? What do you want?"

"You."

"Me? Why? What did I do?"

"You're helping him. I've been told to take you out to send a message to him that they're not fooling around." He pulled tighter on her hair, her hands trying to stop him. "You're become a problem that needs eliminating.

"No, I'm not. I don't know what they told you, but I'm not the one you're after. There's someone who looks a lot like me. She's the one you want."

The man gave a cruel laugh. "Nope. We work together. So, you see, you're wrong."

"But who is after me? I don't understand."

"The ones who want the manuscript information from him." The man's words died away as he looked up and saw the officers surrounding him, weapons pointed at him. His own weapon came up to jam against Larkin's head, causing her to whimper once more in fear. "Back away or she dies."

"I don't think so." Doug's voice in the man's ear brought his head around as he felt Doug's weapon digging into his back. "Let her go."

"She dies first."

"And so do you." Doug nodded towards the team. "You've hurt a police officer. Do you think they'll care if you die?"

The man laughed. "That's not very Christian of you."

"No? Well, guess what. It's your choice if you live or die. But she lives."

Larkin suddenly went limp, her body slipping towards the ground, throwing the man off balance. Doug took him down, his hand reaching to release her hair from the man's grip. He rose, reaching for Larkin as she scurried away from her assailant and drew her to her feet, his arm around her as he ran with her towards the van, shoving her inside.

Caleb reached to draw her down into a chair, finding a blanket to wrap around her, his eyes seeking Frankie.

"Are you okay, Larkin?"

She nodded, fear on her face. "Tierney?"

"He's safe. Ben has him at the department. Are you sure you're okay?"

She nodded again. "I am. But Frankie. He's hurt."

"He was wearing his body armour. If he was hit in the chest, it likely just knocked him down and out for a moment." He watched as Frankie sat up, rubbing at his wrists. "He's up, Larkin."

"He is?" She shifted so she could see. "I'm sorry, Caleb. I'm sorry he was hurt because of me."

"It's not your fault."

"But it is. If I hadn't come to town, he wouldn't have been hurt."

"That's not true. He could have been hurt in any number of ways. It's what we do, Larkin, putting our lives on the line for our people."

Frankie stood at the open van doors, listening to Caleb, his eyes on Larkin, a hand rubbing at his chest. "Caleb's right, Larkin. It could happen at any time. It's a given with the work we do." He reached for her hand. "Caleb, can we get her to the department? She needs Tierney."

Caleb nodded as he jumped down from the van, his eyes searching before he beckoned an officer over. "Lewis? Your vehicle? We need to get Frankie and Larkin to the department."

"Right over here." He walked behind Frankie and Larkin, a hand on his weapon as he searched the area.

Frankie's hand on her back propelled Larkin through the parking lot and into the back door of the building and then down the hall to the conference room. He nodded at Ben who stood in the doorway.

"She's safe?"

"Now she is."

Larkin looked up at Ben. "He was hurt, Ben. He was shot. Make sure he's checked out."

Ben shot Frankie a look, who shook his head. "We will, Larkin. But in you go. Someone's waiting for you."

Tierney spun as he heard Larkin's voice and was across the room with her wrapped into his arms before she had barely stepped into the room. He felt her body shaking with sobs before he swept her up and looking around, found a chair he could sit in, holding on tight to her as she wept.

She finally looked up, swiping at her face. "You're okay?"

"I am. And you? Did you have an adventure without me?" He smiled tenderly at her.

"I did, and I didn't like it. An assassin found me, shot Frankie, and then tried to kill me. That was way too much adventure for my liking."

"It sounds as if it was. Frankie's okay?"

"He is." She looked up at him. "Is it over, Tierney?"

Caleb spoke from the doorway. "It is, Larkin. With this arrest, we have enough evidence to arrest the leader. We'll keep you both here for a couple of hours until we do that. Then, we'll take you home to your own home."

Larkin relaxed back against Tierney, her hands folding into his, her body stopping its shaking as the adrenalin wore off.

# Chapter 39

Three weeks later, Larkin looked up from her desk in the office as she heard Tierney's voice speaking with someone, a frown covering her face until she saw Caleb, Frankie and Abe behind Tierney. She rose, coming to hug the men, before she was swept to Tierney's side.

"Larkin, my love, they just need to finish off the investigation with us."

"Really? It's over?" Larkin's face lit up with hope.

"It is, Larkin. Now, where can we sit?" Caleb smiled as her, his face relaxing for the first time she thought she had seen.

"How about the kitchen?" She squinted at the clock. "It's almost lunchtime. We can talk while we eat, can't we?"

They nodded, the four men stopping to talk quietly as Larkin slipped away to the kitchen, surprised to see Emma there.

"Emma? I didn't know you were here."

"I had to come, Larkin. I hope you don't mind."

Larkin reached to hug her friend. "I don't, not at all. I'm glad you're here. You have been such a friend and support over the last weeks."

"I don't feel like I did that much. This was a difficult one, you know." Emma's hands reached to help Larkin with the meal, turning as she heard the men's voices.

Finally, Caleb sat back, his hand wrapped around a mug of tea, his eyes watching Larkin and Tierney.

"Where would you like us to start, Larkin?"

"Wherever you need to." She reached for Tierney's hand, who not satisfied with just that, wrapped an arm around his bride.

"Well, then, how about when Tierney was a baby. Tierney, you said you had evidence that your parents were drug addicts? That is incorrect. They weren't. They were struggling to survive, your father in school at nights, working during the day. Your mother was at home with you. Somehow, one of them discovered that manuscript and what it meant. The men who had it tried to get it back from your father. When they couldn't, they did kill them with a drug overdose, making it appear that it was an accident. We've had their bodies exhumed by court order, related to this investigation, and those were the findings. So the stigma you've lived with is not what you thought. It will take time to overcome that, I know.

"Now, as to the manuscript. From what we can ascertain, a noted mobster had created it, to hide information from the authorities and his enemies. He died before he could use it or let his family know what it all contained. There were numerous rumours over the years about it and what it was all about. Somehow the man who had it given to you obtained it and wanted that information. He didn't care how he went about getting it.

"Now, your connection to Larkin. It's what we suspected. A chance encounter at the basketball game. They saw you together and thought you were friends. That's why they approached Larkin and her cousins to go in and get you away from the man. The ones who did it? A rival of his. The woman who looked like Larkin? She had been made up like that as had the man who pretended to be Frankie." Caleb paused to take a sip of tea.

Frankie took up the tale. "We have arrested everyone. The account numbers did lead to banks overseas and with the help of the authorities, they have been frozen and ceased. The amount numbers into the millions."

"What happens to it?" Tierney's quiet voice finally broke the silence.

"It will be divided among law enforcement departments. We have a special project we plan to use ours for, but that is still in the planning stages."

"Who was behind this?" Larkin finally spoke, her eyes on Tierney as she did so.

Abe shared a look with Emma. "The man in the photo that Larkin thought looked like Tierney. That was a coincidence but he was the leader. A man by the name of Job Slater."

"Job Slater? Why! I know him! He's another manuscript expert or supposed to be." Tierney watched at Abe nodded. "He's the one who prepared the manuscript, isn't he? That's why he wanted it. He thought that if I found the information, I would turn it over to him. Instead it all blew up on him."

---

"That's what he has admitted to. He used you, Tierney. He wanted those millions but had no idea where to find them. He had been given the manuscript in today's form and was asked to turn it into something old. He'll be away for a number of years."

Caleb spoke again. "The assassins were hired by him. He knew you had turned over the manuscript and decided to take revenge against you. He was at the point he no longer cared if he had the account numbers."

After a while, the four left, leaving Tierney to walk through the house, looking for Larkin. He found her outside, sitting on the deck steps, a thoughtful look on her face. He sat beside her, not saying anything, waiting for her to speak.

She finally wrapped her arms around his, her head on his shoulder. "It's over, Tierney. It's finally over."

"It is, my love." He dropped a kiss on the top of her head. "And we survived."

"Survived, but we are battered and broken. I spoke with Greg. He's agreed to meet with me and said he would with you, if you wanted. If not, he suggested Doug's Darcy."

"I think Greg is best." He waited for her to speak. When she didn't, he tilted his head to look down at her face. "We have to make decisions."

She nodded after a while. "We do. I'll pack and leave, Tierney. This marriage was only temporary." She made a movement to stand, unable to do so when he wrapped his arms around her.

"But I don't want you to, my love. You are my heart, my life, my love. I want to grow old with you, if that isn't too cliched to say."

She turned her face to him, her eyes searching his. "You're sure?" At his nod, she sighed, her head going back to his shoulder. "I was afraid, Tierney, my sweet. I was afraid you hadn't meant what you said, that you wouldn't want me, that I needed to leave. I can't. What you said, it goes for me."

They sat for a while, digesting what the other had said before Tierney reached to touch her face, turning her towards him and into his kiss.

His forehead resting against hers, he prayed, asking God's blessing on her, on their marriage, on their lives together.

# *Epilogue*

Six months later, Tierney stood in their living room, his arm around Larkin as she laughed at Logan's nonsense. It had been a long six months, he thought, with both of them dealing with the aftereffects of what they had been through. It would take a while, but at least his nightmares were subsiding. Larkin's touch over his heart always roused him and calmed him. She said his touch on her face did the same for her. They would get there, he thought, with God's help.

Larkin watched her family as they moved around her home. She was glad they were there. It had been a struggle, she thought, to heal their relationships. A lot of conversations had been held and Tierney had been there for each one, offering her his support. Greg had become involved as well and his wisdom and prayers had gone a long way to helping them heal.

Lincoln watched his sister, seeing in the lady in front of him the girl he had adored. His eyes raised to Tierney and he nodded. Lord, he is just right for her. You prepared both of them for each other. Logan watched his brother and seeing his peace about his sister, sighed. It was okay, he thought. They were all married now, deeply in love with their spouses.

Their parents watched their three children, knowing they were happy, but also realizing that their life mates were not who they had chosen but they were who had been prayed for. God, in His wisdom, had chosen each one for the other.

They had all been shocked when Tierney and Larkin had explained why their adventure as they termed it had happened. When asked by Tierney had been taken captive in the first place, Tierney had grinned, shrugged, and commented that it had all been about money. When he didn't cooperate, it had just evolved to what it had. The men responsible were awaiting trial and that was the end of it. Some things Tierney and Larkin had agreed they would not tell anyone.

Larkin finally turned to Tierney, searching his face, and then reaching to kiss his cheek, his eyes turning down to her.

"Thank you, Tierney, for being the man of God you are. You didn't have a good life, as some would count it, but you did have good foster parents who raised you to be who you are."

He hugged her. "Thank you, my love. Now, where do we go from here?"

She shrugged. "God and God alone knows. All I know is I want to walk life's journey with my hand in yours. Is that too much to ask?"

Dear Readers:

Thank you for choosing the story of Tierney and Larkin. I had no idea when I wrote that first sentence exactly where the story was going. As always, the characters dictated what happened and why. We can become trapped in many different types of prisons, some of our own making, but God always has a key to open the door. He never leaves us, never forsakes us. He is the strong tower to which we run, the wings that hid us, the One who calms our storms.

Tierney's difficulty with stress is so common today, especially in anyone who has suffered a trauma of any kind. Emergency responders are also affected by it. My heart breaks for the family affected by PTSD. It is a devastating illness that can be swept under the rug and ignored by health care professionals. This is not right. Thankfully, it is become more and more acceptable to talk about it and deal with it, although there is a long way to go with this.

What storm are you facing today? What stress? What problem? Nothing is too small to hand over to God. That's all He wants - for us to trust Him enough with our problems that we do just that.

God bless each one of you.


Ronna

CPSIA information can be obtained
at www.ICGtesting.com
Printed in the USA
BVHW041035220819
556528BV00016B/2245/P